This is m!

Daughter
of
Magic

Daughter of Magic

TERESA ROMAN

This book is dedicated to my three Js
Who bring magic into my life every day

Chapter 1

AS I FASTENED the button on the back of my dress, I remembered Dad telling me black wasn't my color. He preferred me in happier shades, he used to say. I never did ask which colors he considered happy, but that hardly mattered now. Black was what people wore to funerals, so there was nothing I could do about it.

Damp, chilly air surrounded me and my aunt Katy as we stepped out of the house that morning. It was as if the sun knew that today was the wrong day to come out. My aunt and I sat in silence as she drove to the cemetery where my father's service and burial were to be held.

"Lilli, say something," Katy urged as she parked her car in the empty cemetery parking lot.

She'd been trying to get me to talk for the past three days—ever since I came home to find my dad lifeless in his bed. But what was there to say? Nothing could give me back my father.

It had always just been the two of us—Dad and me. That's probably why we were so close. The realization that I'd never see him again left me alternating between a hollow feeling and a searing pain that stabbed at my chest, making it hard to breathe. The only parent I'd ever known was gone now, leaving me an orphan at barely eighteen.

Orphan. The word tasted vile in my mouth. I turned to look at my aunt. Her eyes were red and puffy, like mine, but I'd been buried too deep in my own grief to pay attention.

"We're early." It was a stupid thing to say, but the only words that came to my mind.

Katy glanced at her watch. "Half an hour, but I expect people will start getting here pretty soon."

"Then we should find somewhere to sit while we wait for them."

We got out of the car and walked through the cemetery's gates. Wooden folding chairs were lined in rows on either side of my father's casket. A few minutes after we sat down, the funeral guests started to arrive. I recognized only a few faces— people my dad knew from town, acquaintances mostly, rather than friends of my reclusive father. Eventually, my closest friends Emma and Tim arrived, holding hands. The three of us had known each since grade school, but ever since they'd decided they were head over heels for each other, we hadn't spent as much time together.

Emma took my hands in hers and gave them a soft squeeze. "You okay, girl?"

I nodded and bit the inside of my lip, afraid if I answered her I'd start to cry. Tim patted my back before he and Emma went to find a seat. I looked over both shoulders, craning my neck to look for Devin, the one person I wanted to see, but he hadn't shown up yet.

Something else caught my attention—a woman standing off in the distance right by the line of trees flanking the cemetery. Long dark hair fell down over her shoulders. With her head bowed and her hands covering her face, it looked like she was crying. But if she was here for my father, why was she standing so far away?

Something about her pulled me out of my chair. I needed to see her face, to talk to her, to find out if it was my father or someone else who brought her to the cemetery on what felt like the coldest June day in memory.

I mumbled, "I'll be right back" to Katy and left her alone to greet the guests who trickled in. She was too busy accepting someone's condolences to ask me where I was going. Hesitant, I walked toward the woman. What would I say when I got close? For a second, I thought about turning around. What right did I have to intrude on someone's grief? My feet refused to listen to my head, and I kept walking in her direction, hoping that when she finally noticed me, she wouldn't be startled. I was only a few feet away from her when I heard my name being called.

"Lilli." I recognized Devin's voice but kept going, only sparing him a quick glance. The sound of my name being called must've gotten the woman's attention because she lifted her head and gazed at me. I froze as a jolt of recognition ran through me. My mother stood, tall and straight as the trees at her back, her face exactly the same as in the picture I had stashed in my nightstand drawer.

When I felt Devin's hand on my arm, I looked over my shoulder. Relief flooded through me at the sight of his face. I didn't have time to greet him, though. I needed to talk to my mother, but when I turned my head back in her direction she was gone. I took a few hesitant steps forward, then a few more. I could feel Devin trailing closely behind me. When I reached the spot where she had been standing only moments before, I scanned the trees and tombstones, desperate to catch sight of her once more.

"What are you doing all the way over here?" Devin asked.

"Nothing. I . . ." Puzzled, I wasn't sure what to say. "Did you see the woman who was just standing here? Where did she go?"

Devin shook his head. "No, I didn't see anyone."

"She was just here," I insisted. "You *must* have seen her." My heart pounded like a hammer. It wasn't possible for someone to disappear as quickly as she had.

Devin wrapped his hands around my wrists. "Lilli, I didn't see anyone but you." He stared at me intently and I tried to stem the tears that were beginning to well in my eyes. He pulled me into his arms, perhaps sensing how badly I needed to feel them around me. "Are you okay? You're shaking."

I didn't know what to say. If I asked him about the woman again, he'd think I was crazy. Maybe I was, but I didn't want Devin to know that. So I just nodded and whispered yes.

"I wish I knew what to do." Devin's words came out so softly I barely heard him. I wasn't really sure he intended me to, so I didn't respond. Truthfully, him being here for me was enough. Eventually, Devin dropped his arms from around me and laced his fingers through mine. "C'mon. The funeral is going to start soon." As he led me back toward the rows of chairs lined up near my father's casket, I turned my head for one last look, but there was nothing to see.

Shaken, I made my way back to the empty seat next to my aunt.

"Is everything okay?" she asked.

I nodded.

"What were you doing all the way over by the trees?"

Clearly, she hadn't seen my mother either.

"Nothing. I thought I saw someone I knew."

Thankfully, my aunt didn't ask any more questions and a few minutes later the service began. Devin held my hand as the officiant spoke about the transience of life. My dad wasn't a religious man. I couldn't remember him once setting foot in a church, so I didn't know the man speaking, and it was pretty clear by his words that he didn't know my father, either. I tried to focus on his words, but eventually I gave up and let my mind wander.

Dad never spoke about my mother. It was as if he couldn't bear to think about her. He'd answer my incessant questions with a vague smile, then change the subject, until eventually I gave up asking just to avoid seeing the sadness that flared in his eyes. I had no idea what she looked like until I snooped through a drawer in his dresser and found a photograph.

Even then she was instantly familiar to me. I wore my thick, dark—almost black— hair long and straight; so did she. We had the same fair complexion, the same stormy gray eyes.

I stuck the picture into the back pocket of my pants and kept it in my nightstand drawer.

My father must have known I'd stolen it, but he never said a word. Sometimes I felt guilty about it, but I needed something of hers to hold on to, and that picture was all I had. Every so often, late at night, I placed her on the pillow beside me and told her my secrets, the ones I couldn't tell anyone else in the world.

Now that I was older, the resemblance between us was even stronger. Seeing her was like looking at my own reflection. I had made no mistake. The woman I'd seen was my mother, the same woman who had died almost eighteen years ago.

The funeral passed by in a blur. A string of well-wishers came to offer their condolences afterward. I nodded politely and said thank you every time someone told me they were sorry for my loss. After the cemetery cleared out, Devin and I got up.

"Thank you for coming," Katy said to him giving him a quick hug.

"Of course." Devin's eyes met hers, his full of regret. "You know Mark meant a lot to me."

Devin was the first friend I'd had who didn't seem nervous around my dad. My father was a quiet, brooding man, qualities that people mistook for unfriendliness. But in reality his heart was big—and broken. According to Katy, it had been that way since my mother died. People tended to shy away from his often somber moods, but when I introduced Devin to him a few months ago, the two of them somehow connected.

That wasn't the only thing unexpected about Devin. The fact that we were friends at all still surprised to me. We met at a local coffee shop where I was scanning the bulletin board for help wanted flyers. He noticed and asked if I was looking for a job. When I told him I was, he promised he could get me one at the hotel where he worked. I was skeptical, but true to his word, a few days later I got hired.

Working together gave us lots of time to talk and get to know each other, but still, it was unlike me to get close to someone that quickly. I chalked it up to him being the first person my age I got to know outside of school, where I had the reputation of being the shy, weird girl. Devin didn't know that about me, which made it easier to relax around him. He made me smile and laugh, something I didn't do easily. Sometimes it felt like he could see inside of me. Whatever he found he kept to himself, sparing me only the briefest of knowing looks.

Devin reached for my hand. I didn't realize how cold my fingers were until I felt his warmth. "How are you doing?"

"I'm all right." It wasn't true. I hadn't been all right even before I saw—what?— my mother's ghost crying her eyes out at my father's funeral. But I couldn't admit that I was losing my mind, not even to Devin.

"I can go back to your house with you," he offered.

"No." I didn't want to do that to him. I couldn't smile and laugh, much less talk the way we usually did. This wasn't the version of me I wanted him to know.

"Then tell me what I can do."

"Nothing. You being here is enough."

"Are you sure?"

"Yeah. I have Katy. I'll be fine."

Devin dropped my hand. "When will I see you?"

"I don't know."

I shivered as the wind picked up. Katy put her arm around my shoulder.

"You'll call me if you need anything? Even if it's just to talk?" he asked.

I nodded and Devin planted a kiss on my forehead. He stared at me for a moment before walking away.

When he was gone, I turned to look at my father's casket. My chest felt tight, like I had to gasp for air. I walked over and rested my hand along the smooth wooden finish. I would never, ever see my father again. Soon, he would be lowered into the ground, and covered with a mound of dirt. Feeling too weak to hold myself up any longer, I sank to my knees. The earth was cold beneath my legs and I began to shiver again, but I didn't want to leave my dad's side. I curled up into a ball next to the casket, shaking with sobs. Katy kneeled beside me. She draped her sweater over my shoulders, then her arm. The two of us stayed there like that for a long time. Finally, Katy got up and then lifted me to my feet.

"It's time to go home," she said.

Chapter 2

NIGHT BROUGHT AN escape from my aunt's endless hovering. She meant well, trying to get me to eat and asking me for the one hundredth time if I was okay, but I didn't feel like eating and I doubted if I'd ever be okay again. I couldn't tell her that, though.

I lay in bed—half of me desperate for sleep so I could escape the sorrow that wrapped itself around me. The other half worried I'd have another one of my crazy dreams. I already felt like I was perched on the brink of insanity. I couldn't handle my father's funeral, my mother's ghost, and another nightmare about monsters and death all in the same day.

I flashed back to the funeral and tried convincing myself that the woman I saw wasn't my mother. How could she be? She was dead, and I didn't believe in ghosts. Although it wouldn't have been the first time I saw something no one else did.

Maybe it was one of her relatives, someone who'd known my dad and came to grieve. But no matter how hard I tried convincing myself, I knew that wasn't right. If my mother had relatives, I would've already met them by now. My mother's family, if she had one, was as much a mystery as she was.

Katy was all I had left, but she lived in Eureka, more than an hour away. My aunt and her boyfriend had been together for a long time, but Katy didn't believe in marriage and they'd never had any kids. That meant a cousin wasn't in the cards for me, no matter how badly I wanted one.

I wondered what Katy would think if I said anything about what I'd seen at the funeral earlier. There was no way I could. She worried too much about me already. Even though she didn't have kids of her own, she had a natural sense of what I needed. Over the years, I'd overheard enough conversations between her and my dad to know that without her, my dad wouldn't have had a clue how to raise a girl.

Between the attention I received from Dad and Katy, I never really thought about my mother until I started kindergarten. That's when I noticed that I was the only kid who didn't have someone to call Mommy. Since my dad never mentioned her, I assumed the worst—that she'd run away because she didn't want a child. After thinking about it for so long that I couldn't keep my thoughts bottled up any longer, I worked up the courage to talk to Katy. She'd come up to spend the long Thanksgiving weekend with us, and even though it was already getting cold out, I begged her to take me to get ice cream. My dad had stayed home to catch up on work, which gave me the chance to ask Katy the question that had been on my mind since school started.

"Why don't I have a mother?" I asked. "Is it because she didn't want me?"

Katy's face blanched before she tried to explain. "No, Lilli! It had nothing to do with you."

"Then what happened to her?"

My aunt looked away for a minute, like she was deciding

whether or not to tell me the truth. Finally she said, quietly, "Nobody really knows for sure. When you were still a baby, she just vanished one day. She went out to run some errands and never came back. Your father looked everywhere for her, so did his friends, and the police. But no one ever found her."

"What happened to her?" I repeated, not understanding.

"I think the angels took her," Katy replied. "We don't know how or why, but that's what happened, because if she were still alive, she would be with you and your dad. She loved the two of you very much."

"So I'll never see her?" I asked, trying to hold back tears.

Katy hesitated before answering. "No. I'm sorry, but you won't."

"Dad doesn't think she's dead. He thinks she's going to come back."

"What makes you say that?" Katy asked, frowning. "Did your dad tell you that?"

"No," I said, shrugging my shoulders, not sure why Katy was bothered so much by what I had said. "I can just tell."

"I know your dad wants her to come back, but sometimes we don't get what we want." Katy reached for my hand. "You understand that, don't you?"

Knowing how heart-broken losing my mother had left Dad, I did my best to make him proud. He never had to get after me about doing chores or my homework. I earned good grades and never got into trouble. I didn't experiment with alcohol or drugs, not even cigarettes. I lived for the moments I could bring a smile to his face, like when I brought a report card home, or when someone commented on what a well-behaved daughter he had.

But despite my determination, I was far from the perfect

child. Without meaning to, I gave my dad plenty to worry about, and it all started right after Katy explained what happened to my mother. I woke up screaming one night after dreaming about people being burned alive. Dad didn't seem too concerned at first, but when the nightmares continued, he took me to see a psychologist.

Talking about the dreams didn't help. They still came, thankfully not every night, but when they did, they were horrifying. I watched helplessly as people were tortured, drowned, burned.

Then the scenarios changed. For a while, my dreams were actually kind of cool. I dreamt about people who could control fire and wind and do all sorts of magic. But despite their enormous power, they weren't invincible. They had enemies, monsters who appeared human but then morphed into something beastly before attacking. Not all of the monsters looked the same. Some had talon-like fingers, and others had goat-like horns. Often, they had contorted facial features and fangs for teeth, but they were all similar in one way, they had eyes as black as pitch and they scared me. Once again, my screams woke Dad in the middle of the night.

I felt guilty that my father was almost as sleep deprived as I was, but things got worse when I saw one of the monsters from my dreams—in real life. Dad was used to hearing me cry out in the night, but not when the two of us were out in public. He brought me back to the psychologist, and, when I explained what happened, he told my father I needed to be medicated. Dad refused, vowing to find another way to help me, and never took me to another doctor. I became just as afraid of seeing another monster as I was of upsetting my dad, so I learned how to control my reaction to them. Instead of screaming, I turned my head and found an excuse to leave wherever I was. It became obvious after a while that I was the only one seeing them. But even though I'd managed to convince my dad that everything was fine, it wasn't. And now, after seeing my mother today, I worried that I was getting worse, and I was doing it alone, without anyone around to help.

By three in the morning, I was still awake. I got up, went to the bathroom and rummaged through the medicine cabinet looking for the sleeping pills Katy had been giving me the past few nights. They were the only thing that seemed to help, and somehow they kept my strange dreams at bay.

By the time I woke up the next morning, it was ten o'clock. I made my way downstairs and found my aunt looking through some papers.

"I'm glad you got some sleep," she said. "There's some breakfast in the kitchen for you."

"I'm not hungry," I mumbled.

She gave me an exasperated look.

"What are those?" I asked as I sat beside her on the couch.

"Legal stuff," she replied. "Your father's will and some other paperwork he left behind."

"Why are you looking at that now?"

My aunt sighed and moved the papers off her lap. "Unfortunately, there is a lot to think about after someone dies, and since you and I are pretty much Mark's only relatives that leaves me with the responsibility."

Technically, we weren't my dad's only relatives. His parents were still alive. They'd moved to Arizona just after my grandfather retired to escape the cold damp Northern California weather. They lived in an assisted living facility and were too frail to take long trips. Dad and I visited them once a year. My grandmother had hip problems and used a wheel-chair, and over the past few years my grandfather had gotten to the point where he didn't even remember who Dad and I were half the time.

"Is there something I can do?"

"No." Katy shook her head. "Most of this legal mumbo jumbo is too hard for even me to figure out. You can take a look at this if you want though."

Katy handed me a thick sheaf of papers. *Last Will and Testament*, it read at the top of the page. I glanced over it, but my aunt was right. It was full of words I barely understood.

"Basically what it says is that your father left you this house. It's completely paid for. He left you some money, too. It's not enough to live off forever, but it's a good amount, and it'll help you pay your way through college whenever you decide to go."

Suddenly, I felt weary. I wasn't supposed to be thinking about things like this. I was supposed to be worrying about what to wear to stupid frat parties, but I'd put off going to college and stuck around Crescent City because I liked my job at the hotel. Now I wasn't even sure I wanted to go to college anymore. It was too much to think about.

"Can we talk about this later?"

"Sure, of course," Katy replied. She picked the papers back up and shuffled them nervously in her hands. "There's no rush."

I made my way into the kitchen and managed to eat a few bites of toast. The sun had come out and I suddenly longed to feel its warmth on my skin. I sat outside on my front stoop, still in my pajamas, and stared at the street, counting the cars that drove by. The mindlessness of it kept me from thinking for a bit, but eventually my brain slipped back into instant replay.

Less than a week ago, Devin and I had spent the morning at Ocean World—an aquarium, and one of Crescent City's biggest tourist attractions. Devin picked me up at my house that morning. He came inside to talk to my dad first—neither of us noticed anything unusual. Ocean World was a pretty cool place, with a sea lion show and a shark-petting tank. I'd been there a hundred times before, especially when I was a kid, but it was Devin's first visit. I pretended to be a tour guide, and Devin played right along, asking me the types of questions I imagined our hotel guests would.

A few hours later, Devin and I returned home with Mexican take-out. I looked for my dad downstairs in his office. When there was no sign of him there, I went to his bedroom. At first I thought he was asleep, until I noticed his pale skin and blue lips. I couldn't find a pulse and must have screamed, because Devin came running. He took one look at my dad and knew what I was unwilling to accept. He pulled me into my arms and held me while I sobbed, his shirt soaking up my tears. If Devin hadn't been there, I don't know what I would've done.

Katy drove up from Eureka that same day. I was a mess by the time she arrived, insisting that it was my fault Dad had died—if only I hadn't gone to Ocean World with Devin, then maybe he'd still be alive. Guilt ate at me even after the coroner told us my father had experienced a sudden cardiac event. I couldn't have prevented it.

Even so, he had died alone—and maybe frightened. It had become one more thought that got added to the list of things I couldn't wipe from my mind.

Chapter 3

THE NEXT FEW days passed in a blur. I went through the normal motions of life—sleeping, eating, watching television, even though normal was the last thing I felt. Somehow, a week went by since my father's funeral.

One afternoon as I sat at the kitchen table, gazing into the backyard, my phone rang. The sandwich Katy had made earlier for me sat untouched on my plate. She stared at me like she did every time I ignored my phone. I wasn't in the mood for conversation and didn't even bother to check caller ID. This time Katy let out a loud sigh, snapping me out of my trance.

"That's it," she said, her voice unusually firm. "It's time you and I had a talk. A *real* talk."

"What do you want to talk about?" I asked, trying to sound animated enough to convince her there was no need for a *real* talk.

"I think you should stay with me for a while," she said bluntly.

I sighed and shook my head. "We've already discussed that." I told Katy no a few days ago when she suggested I

move to Eureka and live with her. I was eighteen, had been for a few weeks, so it was my decision to make. "I want to live here."

"Look at me."

I lifted my eyes and gazed at her, even though it hurt to do so. She looked so much like Dad that it made my heart ache. Same sandy brown hair, same hazel eyes. I didn't look a thing like either of them, although Katy often said Dad and I had similar personalities.

"I'm worried about you being here by yourself. You're not eating, and you're barely sleeping. Who's going to take care of you when I'm gone?"

"I can take care of myself."

My aunt shook her head. "No, I don't think you can." Her sympathetic tone had vanished, and she sounded like she meant business. I braced myself for what was coming. "Losing Mark was bad enough, but seeing you like this is too much. I can't stand it."

"Dad died a few days ago. What is it you're expecting, that I just act like nothing happened?"

"No, of course not . . ."

"I miss him, that's all. I would expect you, of all people, to understand."

"I do. But sitting around the house starving yourself isn't going to bring him back."

She reached for my hand.

I looked down and bit the inside of my cheek to keep from crying. "I should've been with him."

"Honey, you can't change what happened. No one can. What you're going through, losing your father, finding him like you did, that would be hard for anyone."

"What am I supposed to do?" I stood up, walked over to the window and crossed my arms in front of my chest. "A part of me wishes I could forget, but then another part of me gets angry for feeling that way. I don't want to forget the good parts, just . . ." I shook my head. "There's just some things I wish I could get out of my mind."

"What if I took you to grief counseling? Would you be willing to give that a try?"

"No way, I won't go."

Surely, Katy had to remember what a bad experience it had been for me when Dad brought me to the psychologist as a kid.

"Then at least talk to me," she said. "Tell me what I can do to help."

"There's nothing you can do, Katy. I know you miss Dad, too, but it's different for you." A tear rolled down my face, and I swiped it away with the back of my hand. "He's all I had."

"I've tried to be here as much as I could."

"I know, Katy. You've done so much for me, and I . . . I really do appreciate it." My shoulders slumped in defeat. Maybe if I confessed to Katy that it wasn't only Dad's death that had me feeling so hopeless, she'd back off about me moving to Eureka or going to counseling. "It's just that I haven't been sleeping well. Even before Dad died. I was still getting those creepy dreams. Now they're coming more often, and I've . . . been thinking about my mother." There was no way I could tell Katy that I'd actually seen her.

"Given everything that's happened, I think it's perfectly natural that you'd be thinking about her. I just wish you would've told me sooner," Katy said. "And as far as the dreams go, maybe they'll get better if you talk to someone about them."

"Oh, please, Aunt Katy. Not this again."

"Then tell me what to do. Tell me how I can help you."

"I don't know how to do this." I shook my head. "I don't know how to be alone."

Katy stood and walked over to me. She laid a hand on my shoulder. "You're not alone. You have me and you have your friends."

The doorbell rang. Neither of us expected visitors.

Katy patted my shoulder and went to answer the door.

"Speak of the devil," she said.

"The devil?" Devin stepped inside.

"Of course you're not the devil," my aunt said, sounding flustered. "It's just an expression."

"Glad to hear it," he teased.

Their exchange brought a smile to my face. Devin had an uncanny ability to charm my aunt despite their twenty-year age difference. She wasn't the only one, either. It was partly how handsome he was. His eyes were an impossibly striking color—not blue, not green, but a shade in between that reminded me of the ocean. They lit up whenever he smiled. Wavy mahogany hair complemented his slightly tan complexion. He stood a few inches taller than I did and had strong broad shoulders. But it wasn't just the way he looked that made him so appealing. There was something else, something compelling I didn't know how to put into words.

"I'll leave the two of you alone," Katy said before climbing the stairs.

Devin walked over and wrapped his arms around my

waist. I leaned into him and the two of us stood there without talking for a few moments.

"Everyone's missed you at work," Devin finally said.

"By everyone do you mean you?"

"No. Rob and Angela have been asking about you, too. But you're right, it's different for me. You're . . . my friend; I feel like I can't doing anything right without you."

It was hard to believe that could be true, although more and more I'd begun to feel the same way about him. At first I chalked it up to the fact that ever since I'd graduated a few weeks ago and increased my hours at the hotel we'd spent so much more time around each other. But deep down, I knew that wasn't the reason. "Do I even still have my job?"

"Of course you do. Rob wouldn't dream of firing you at a time like this. I'd break his legs if he did."

I took a step back and Devin's arms fell to his side. "Why are you always trying to be my hero?"

"Everybody needs a hero, Lilli. I want to be yours. You just have to let me." He reached out to brush my hair over my shoulder.

I didn't know what to make of his words. I wanted them to mean something—that he'd begun to feel about me the way I did for him. But it was probably wishful thinking. Knowing Devin, the reason for his extra kindness was because of what happened to my father.

"After all the things you've done for me, I think you hit hero status quite a while ago." I kept my voice light, even though I meant every word. Not only did he get me a job— not an easy feat in Crescent City where unemployment was rampant—but he was the first person besides my aunt that I ever felt comfortable talking to about my mother. And if he hadn't been with me when I found my dad, I don't know how I ever would've gotten past the shock.

He lifted my chin and looked into my eyes. "You've been crying." His hand moved to my cheek. "I'm sorry, that was a stupid thing to say; of course you've been crying."

Staring into Devin's eyes, feeling his hand on my cheek, made me feel better and worse at the same time. He had no idea how impossibly hard it was to be around him when all I wanted was for him to kiss me, to tell me he needed me as badly as I did him. I lowered my gaze and he dropped his hand.

"When are you coming back to work?" he asked.

"Tomorrow, I think." The words just came out. But after I said them I knew it was the right answer. I'd already taken almost two weeks off, any longer and I might not have a job to come back to. Somehow, Katy's talk had managed to convince me that I couldn't sit around the house in my pajamas forever.

"Thank goodness." Devin smiled, bringing out the sparkle in his eyes that made me tremble inside. "You have no idea how tired I'm getting of Angela and her half hour smoke breaks. It's bad enough she leaves me alone at the front desk, then she comes back smelling like an ashtray." He paused when he reached his objective—a smile on my face. "Can you do me a favor?"

"That depends."

"Can you try and get some sleep?"

A good night's sleep wasn't something I could promise anyone. I hadn't told Devin about my dreams and my visions. I'd been tempted to a few times, just to get it off my chest, but then I worried that he'd think of me as crazy. I doubted he'd be interested in me then.

"I'll do my best."

"Okay, well, I guess that's all I can ask for." He gave me another hug. "I should get going. I just wanted to come by and make sure you were okay, since you apparently forgot how to answer a phone."

"I'm sorry. It's just that . . ."

"It's okay, I understand." Devin kissed me on the cheek. "Just take care of yourself, Lilli," he said before turning to leave.

Chapter 4

THAT NIGHT, WHILE I lay in bed, I thought about what Katy had said. Life went on. Dad wouldn't want me to spend it the way I had been since he died. I still couldn't erase the image of my mother crying at Dad's funeral, but I'd done a good job of explaining it to myself in a way that made sense. We were at a cemetery. If I were to see a ghost anywhere, that would be the place. I still had no explanation for my crazy dreams, but I'd been having them for so long that I doubted I would ever have an answer. If only I could figure out a way to get used to them.

Over breakfast the next morning, Katy tried to convince me again to move in with her.

"I don't like you staying here alone," she said after I gave her my answer, "but you're eighteen, so I guess there's nothing I can do."

"I'll be fine."

She sighed, and thankfully dropped the subject. "I'll come back and visit as soon as I can."

As I watched her drive off, I pushed back against the sadness that washed over me. With Katy gone, I'd be coming home to an empty house. The thought of it upset me so much that I almost changed my mind about going to work, but staying home all day seemed like a worse option.

The sun broke through the clouds early that morning and lifted my mood as I drove to work. Summer brought a lot of tourists to Crescent City. People liked to vacation here where the air was almost always twenty degrees cooler than everywhere else.

The Tides Inn was a small hotel, not what anyone would consider fancy. Crescent City didn't really do fancy, but it was along the coast and some rooms even had oceanfront views. Crescent City was known for its beautiful shoreline and amazing redwood forests. People came for kayaking and fishing and miles of hiking trails, but aside from that, there wasn't much to the actual town. Downtown was tiny, just a few shops and restaurants, and looked pretty run-down, earning the nickname "Cretin City" from a few unhappy locals.

Devin was already behind the front desk when I showed up. He was talking to Rob, our manager. They both turned their heads in my direction as I walked through the door.

"I'm glad you're back," Rob said, as I ducked under the desk partition to join them.

"Thanks."

"I'm so sorry for your loss."

"Thank you."

"I should get going. I've got a stack of paperwork in my office that I need to tackle." Rob left through the back exit.

"For a while there, I thought you weren't going to come," Devin said.

"Why?" I glanced at the clock. It was five minutes before nine. "I'm not late."

"You're usually here a lot earlier. I was starting to worry that you changed your mind about being ready to come back to work."

"Katy left this morning," I explained.

A look of shock spread across Devin's face. "She left you alone?"

"She has a job, a life, she can't exactly stay here forever."

"Yes, but you're . . ."

I put my hands on my hips, bracing myself for what Devin was about to say. He never finished his sentence.

"I'm what? Only eighteen—is that what you were going to say?"

"No, but that is a good point."

"You live on your own."

"That's different."

"Really? How?"

"I'm older than you, for one thing, and I'm . . ."

"You're a year older than me." I came to a sudden realization and narrowed my eyes at Devin. "Please don't tell me this is about me being a girl."

"It's not, and it isn't about you being eighteen, either. The world can be a dangerous place, Lilli."

"And what would you have me do?" I asked, trying not to get upset. It wasn't like I asked to be on my own, after all. "I don't exactly have many other choices." I silently prayed he wouldn't suggest that I move to Eureka to be with my aunt. That would crush me.

"Move in with me," Devin blurted out.

I stared at him, my mouth open wide, but before I got a chance to respond, the lobby door swung open and a hotel guest walked in with his room card in hand. After I finished checking him out, another guest strolled in, then another. It stayed busy until almost noon. I snuck out for my lunch break, alone, to think about Devin's offer.

Moving in with him was a good idea, in theory. I didn't relish the idea of being in my house alone. There were too many memories there. I didn't know how I was supposed to not think about the fact that my dad died in his bedroom just a few feet down the hall from mine. But my feelings for Devin were too confusing. They had been that way almost from the time we met, and, as the months went by, I never succeeded in talking myself out of what I felt. There were times I wondered if maybe he felt something for me, too. I fantasized that the reason he helped me get hired at the Tides was because, when he spotted me in the coffee shop, he thought I was pretty and wanted to get to know me better. I mean, who offers to help a random stranger get a job without some sort of ulterior motive? But if he had one, I never figured out what it was.

When I returned from my lunch break, the lobby was empty. As I joined Devin behind the desk, he said, "So did you think about what I asked earlier?"

"Isn't it your turn to go on a break?" I replied, not eager to have this conversation with him.

"I'm not going anywhere until you tell me yes."

"You don't want a roommate, trust me. I'll drive you crazy."

Devin stared at me, unwavering. "Not possible."

"It's not that I don't want to," I began. It felt weird rejecting something I really wanted to accept. "It's just that . . . I just can't."

"Is it because of work? You think we spend too much time together?"

"No," I replied too quickly. There was no way I could get him to understand without saying too much, and I couldn't do that. There was only so much heartbreak I could take at one time.

"Then why?"

"So much has changed in my life. Right now, I just need one thing to stay the same."

Devin's jaw tensed, but if it did because he was unhappy with my answer, he kept it to himself. Instead, he said, "Then at least come over tonight after work. Can you do that?"

I managed a smile. "I guess I can."

After work, I followed Devin back to his place in my car. He lived in a small, one-story rental property. I hadn't been over in a few weeks, but nothing about the inside had changed. His home was the tidiest and least cluttered place I'd ever seen. He had no family photos dotting the walls, no memorabilia lining the bookshelf in his living room. I'd asked him about that once and received only a vague reply. He was good at giving those, but every time I tried digging deeper, I hit a brick wall. I swore to myself that one day I'd get him to break down and tell me his secrets.

"Take a seat." Devin gestured toward the couch as he closed the door behind us. "Are you hungry?" he asked, as he made his way toward the kitchen.

"A little."

"Give me a few minutes and I'll have dinner ready."

"You don't need to cook," I said, as I listened to him rummage through his kitchen cabinets. "We can just order pizza."

He poked his head into the living room. "You're kidding me, right?" Devin didn't like fast food. An aversion he and my dad shared. His cooking amazed; the dishes he prepared were simple, but tasted magnificent. Devin seemed to be one of those people who did everything well.

After a few minutes the smells coming from the kitchen made my mouth water. I hadn't realized how hungry I was. I joined Devin in the kitchen. "Let me help," I said.

"No need. You just sit and relax. I'll be done soon."

"I can at least set the table."

He reached into the cabinet above him and handed me two plates. By the time I finished laying the forks down beside the dishes, Devin came from the kitchen with a large tray in his hands. He set it down in the center of the table and we both sat. Normally, I wasn't much of a salad person, but he'd made a dressing that I couldn't get enough of. Besides salad, Devin had pan-fried fish. Moist and flaky, the fish had the slightest hint of lemon and butter and practically melted in my mouth.

Eating dinner together brought back memories of my dad. I remembered the first time Devin cooked a meal at my house. Dad had been so impressed.

I was so deep in thought that I didn't realize I'd stopped eating. "What are you thinking about?" Devin asked.

"Dad," I said, unable to hide the longing in my voice, "and the first time you cooked for us."

"I'm sorry. I didn't mean to . . ."

"It's not your fault. It's not anybody's."

"I miss him, too."

For some reason it felt good to hear him say that. "I'm sorry," I said, picking up my fork. "I didn't mean to ruin dinner."

"You didn't ruin anything." Devin leaned forward and

reached for my hand. "I just don't like to see you sad . . . and I really hate the idea of you being all by yourself."

I gave him a weak smile. "You worry too much."

Sometimes, I liked Devin's overprotectiveness, figuring if he didn't care, he wouldn't fret over me as much as he did. He got on my case all the time about locking doors and being more aware of my surroundings. I didn't tell him that sometimes I purposely tried *not* to be aware of what was going on around me. The less I paid attention to faces, the smaller the chance that I'd see one that frightened me and made me question my sanity. "I'll be fine."

"At least promise me something?"

I shrugged and said okay.

"If you need me, you'll call, even if it's just to talk, no matter what time it is?"

"Yeah, of course." Although I doubted it would ever come to that. I'd always been pretty self-sufficient and hated dumping on other people. Besides, my problems weren't exactly the type I could share, at least not if I wanted to remain outside the walls of a mental hospital.

After we finished eating, I helped Devin clean up and then the two of us sat back down on the couch. I turned the TV on. Devin had no cable, and not much was on except for the local news, which in Crescent City wasn't very exciting.

"You should seriously consider getting cable," I said after finding nothing of interest to watch.

"I have some movies." Devin got up and returned with a box in his hands. The movies were ancient and probably left behind by the last renter. I managed to find something that looked like it might be funny and popped it into the DVD player.

Soon after it started, the sky began to darken. It was still early, barely after eight, but my eyelids grew heavy. All those sleepless nights had caught up with me. Devin wrapped his arm around my shoulders and pulled me closer. He smelled good, earthy, like the herbs my dad grew in his garden. A mix of lavender and rosemary. The warmth of his body comforted me, and before long I drifted off to sleep.

It was the worst time to have another one of my dreams.

Chapter 5

I STOOD IN A field surrounded by shades of blue and green. The sky was nearly cloudless, the blades of grass under my feet were soft and plush like a carpet, and the trees in the distance swayed in the gentle breeze. I took in the idyllic scene and, at first, saw no one. Then I heard a man's voice, followed by a woman's, then soft laughter that could only belong to a child. I walked toward the sound until I stood only a few feet away from the couple playing with their son. They were in a courtyard that stood in the center of a building that took up three sides of a square. The building was flanked by enormous statues that looked like lions with wings.

Suddenly, the sky darkened and three men appeared out of nowhere.

The man lifted his son into his wife's arms. "Take him and go."

"No," she said. "We're staying with you."

One of the men laughed, his coal black eyes full of evil, then his faced morphed into something monstrous. His eyes receded while his forehead became more prominent, the complexion of his skin taking a slightly greenish hue. Teeth sharpened into fangs and, from his fingers, talons grew. "More witches for us to kill."

"Go," the man roared again. But his wife refused to listen.

Everything happened so quickly. The man, his wife who held their son in her arms, and the monsters vanished and reappeared so quickly I could barely tell who was who and what was happening until I heard the woman scream. I wanted to do something, but I felt frozen, helpless. The woman fell to the ground, throwing herself over her son's body, but not before turning to thrust a dagger into one of the creature's chests. As the dagger went in, the creature fell backward, his body turning into a pile of ash. Two more piles of ash littered the courtyard, along with the man's body. It lay in a heap only feet away from the woman and their son.

"No," I cried out at the sight of the man's body, but my distress was nothing compared to the anguish of his wife and child. As their cries filled the air, my heart bled for them. "No," I cried out again as I choked back a sob. They couldn't hear me.

Out of nowhere, hands wrapped around my arms. I gasped as shock and fear coursed through me, sure that another one of those monsters had returned, except this time it could see me. I jerked my arms wildly in an effort to free myself from its grip.

The next thing I knew I was awake, shaking, with tears streaming down my face.

Devin pulled me into his arms. "Lilli, what's happening?"

"He's dead," I said before I could stop myself. "They killed him in front of his family."

"Who's dead?"

"I don't know."

"It was just a dream, Lilli."

My racing heart began to slow. The hands wrapped around my arms were Devin's. He'd been trying to wake me up.

"I'm sorry." I pulled away and wiped my tears. "This is so embarrassing."

For a few moments, neither of us said anything. Then Devin reached across to rest his hand on mine. "Can you tell me about it?"

"No, it's stupid."

"Was it about your father?"

I shook my head, willing the subject of my nightmare to go away, but I knew that Devin wouldn't let it go so easily.

"Then what?"

"I don't want to talk about it." I stood and looked around the room, trying to remember where I'd left my bag. Devin reached for my hand again.

"Where do you think you're going?"

"Home; it's late."

"You are *not* going anywhere."

My shaky legs weren't strong enough to keep me on my feet with Devin tugging on my hand. I landed back on the couch beside him.

"I want you to tell me what your dream was about. I might be able to help."

"I don't need help. Like I said, it was just a bad dream, no big deal."

"Bad dreams don't leave people screaming and shaking."

I turned my head away from him. "If I tell you, you'll think I'm crazy."

"I won't. Nothing you can say will make me think that way." He sounded so sure of himself.

"You only say that because you don't know."

"Don't know what?"

"How seriously messed up I am."

"Hey." Devin scooted closer to me and grasped my chin with his hand, turning my head so that I faced him. "Don't ever say that about yourself."

I shook my head free.

"Don't you trust me, Lilli? I know that I can help with whatever's bothering you if you only let me."

Despite the voice in my head that shouted at me to keep my secrets to myself, the need to unburden myself was stronger. I rested my elbows on my knees and lowered my face into my open hands. With my heart pounding again, I began to tell Devin about my dream. "I saw a man die in front of his family. He was killed by something . . . something evil. There were three of them, some kind of monster looking things. I don't know what they were, but they turned into ash after they died. Vampires do that, don't they? It was daytime, though. Aren't vampires supposed to sleep during the day?"

I wasn't sure what reaction to expect from Devin after my insane rambling, but he surprised me, when sounding both certain and sincere he said, "They weren't vampires."

I let everything that had been on my chest for so long spill out. "I've been having nightmares ever since I was a kid. Not normal ones, either. I dream about witches and magic and monsters and people dying, and all I do is stand there and watch because there's nothing I can do to stop it. I think if I knew they were just dreams I could stand it, but they don't feel like dreams; they feel like something else. I know this sounds crazy, but it feels like I'm having visions of things that have really happened. Only that's impossible because witches and magic and monsters don't exist."

"What if they do?"

I hesitated before continuing. "I don't know. I've never believed in the supernatural. Except, now I'm beginning to wonder if maybe I'm wrong."

"Really?" Devin said, his curiosity piqued. "And why is that?"

I took a deep breath as the memory of my father's funeral flooded my mind. I wasn't ready to tell him about seeing my mother's ghost. Instead, I explained that I'd been coming face to face with the monsters from my dreams.

"Do you think they've ever noticed you the same way you've noticed them?" Devin asked.

His question struck me as strange, although it seemed genuine and not the least bit patronizing. I wasn't sure how he could believe me when half the time I didn't even really believe that what I saw was real. "No. Well, except the first time. I was with my dad and I remember screaming and hiding my head. I was just a little kid then, so I think everyone who heard me crying just figured I was throwing a tantrum. But ever since then, whenever I saw one, I just tried to get away. I'd turn and head in the opposite direction, or tell my dad that I needed to go to the bathroom and run off. He always knew what it meant when I did that."

"You must've been so scared."

"I was. I still am, because I never know when it's going to happen. I can go months without seeing one, but then I'll see several of them in a week. And the crazy thing is that I'm pretty sure I'm the only one that sees them, so it's not like I have anyone I can talk to about it."

Devin shook his head before clasping his hands around the back of his neck. "This is why I don't think you should be alone. It's not safe."

It took a minute for his words to sink in. "Are you saying you think what I've been seeing isn't just a product of my imagination?"

"No . . . Yes. I mean, how can anyone ever really be sure about things like this? But why take chances you don't have to?"

I took that to mean that he sort of believed me. Since I was already on a roll, I decided to spill the rest of my story to see how he'd react.

"There's more," I said.

What the hell was I doing?

"What do you mean?"

"I saw my mother's ghost." I waited for a response, but Devin remained quiet. I went on. "I'm scared. I mean, I've gotten sort of used to the dreams and stuff, but I've never seen ghosts before. What if it happens again? I feel like I'm losing my mind."

"You're not losing your mind." Devin stared at his feet, twined his fingers together and held his hands in his lap. He looked up, then down again. It seemed like the only direction he didn't turn his head in was mine. Finally, he said, "Think about it. Considering what you've been through, it's not so strange that you saw your mother at your father's funeral."

Something dawned on me as Devin finished speaking. "Wait a minute. I never told you I saw her at my father's funeral. How did you know?"

"I . . . I just remember that day," Devin stammered. "You

asked me if I saw a woman. I put two and two together just now and assumed that's who you were talking about."

"Please don't tell anyone what I just told you," I pleaded. "I don't want anyone else to think I'm crazy."

"First of all, I won't breathe a word of this to anyone." Devin pressed his hand to the small of my back. I let out a breath I hadn't realized I was holding. "And second of all, I don't think you're crazy."

"So you believe in ghosts?" I asked sarcastically. "And monsters?"

"I believe in a lot of things. Far more than most people do."

"So what you're saying is that we're both crazy?" I felt like laughing, if only to ease the tension. "Maybe that's why we're such good friends."

As Devin scooted closer to me, I turned to look at him again. He clasped the sides of my face in his hands. The only light in the room came from the TV, but it was enough to see that he was staring at me. For a moment, I thought he was going to kiss me. My heart fluttered as I imagined what his lips would feel like on mine. But then he pulled his hand away, turned his head and whispered, "No," under his breath.

"What's wrong?" I asked.

Devin shook his head. "What's wrong is that you need to get some sleep." He stood and held his hand out to me. "Come."

As he pulled me up I asked, "Where are we going?"

"I'm taking you to my bed." Before I could protest, he scooped me into his arms as if I were as light as a feather. Being in his arms, feeling the heat of his body against mine caused my heart to flutter wildly.

I clasped my hands behind his neck.

"I don't think I'll be able to fall back asleep," I said as he carried me down the hallway toward his bedroom.

"I want you to try. Can you do that?" he asked. "I'll stay with you until you do and then I'll go sleep on the couch."

"No. It's your house. I should be the one to sleep on the couch."

"No more arguing with me, Lilli. You need to get some sleep, and you'll do that in my bed where you can get comfortable, not on my lumpy couch."

When we got to his room, he laid me down on his bed and pulled the covers over me. "Close your eyes," he whispered as he sat down beside me on the edge of the bed.

I turned on my side and tried to fall back asleep. It hadn't been my intention to spend the night or to reveal all my secrets to Devin, but it was too late to take anything back. My churning mind kept me awake. Between thinking about the latest dream, my mother, and my dad, I couldn't shut down.

After a few minutes, I felt Devin get up. I turned to see where he was going.

"You're supposed to be sleeping," he said.

"Can you stay with me?"

"Of course." Devin took a seat in the armchair that was wedged in the corner of his room.

"No, not there." I patted the spot on the bed where he'd just been sitting. "Here."

He got up and asked, "Are you sure?"

I nodded and Devin came to sit beside me again. He folded his hands in his lap.

"You can't sleep sitting up." I lifted the covers. Devin hesitated for a moment before sliding in bed beside me. He lifted his arm and I nestled my head on his chest. I felt like I was melting into him, the warmth of his strong chest made me quiver inside. Eventually, my racing heart slowed, and I was finally able to fall asleep.

Chapter 6

I WOKE UP ALONE and feeling out of sorts. Gradually, everything came back to me. I couldn't believe that I'd actually confessed all my secrets to Devin. As if that wasn't bad enough, I'd made him sleep beside me. What had I been thinking? I wanted to throw a pillow over my head and pretend last night never happened, but sunlight burst through the window in Devin's room and beckoned me out of bed. About to peel back the covers, I heard a knock on the door. I probably looked terrible, still wearing the same clothes from the day before: khaki pants and a white polo with the name Tides Inn embroidered in gold thread over the left side of my chest. Even if I wanted to take a shower, I had no change of clothes.

"Come in," I called out.

"Did you sleep all right?" Devin asked as he stepped through the doorway. The smell of pancakes filled the room, making my stomach rumble.

"I did." I threw the covers back and planted my feet on the floor. "Thanks for letting me sleep in your bed."

"Are you feeling better this morning?"

I nodded and tried to hide my embarrassment by looking around the room for my bag. Then I remembered I'd left it in the living room. "But I really should get back home and take a shower."

"You need breakfast first. I made your favorite."

"Blueberry pancakes?" I didn't have to ask, the heavenly aroma of them filled the air.

Devin nodded. Blueberry pancakes were also my dad's favorite. He'd taught Devin how to make them. Cooking was one of the things the two of them bonded over. I remembered watching them in the kitchen together. My dad, the self-proclaimed expert, and Devin, playing the part of the dutiful student. The memory sent a sharp pain through my chest. What I wouldn't give to get those days back.

Distracted and suddenly close to tears, I smoothed my hair. I needed a comb and a toothbrush at the very least before I could feel presentable, but Devin's pleading look was hard to resist, and I never could say no to blueberry pancakes. I wiped my eyes and managed a shaky smile.

"You look beautiful. You always do," Devin said as if he knew what I was worried about.

I blushed. If he thought I was beautiful, what was holding him back? Was I not his type? Girls flirted with him all the time at work, but he showed no interest in them, at least not while I was around. I asked him once if he had a girlfriend waiting for him somewhere. Before telling me no, he laughed and made a self-deprecating remark about not exactly being the type of man anyone waited around for. The fact that he seemed to have no idea how incredibly gorgeous he was somehow made him even more attractive.

After practically inhaling breakfast, I drove back home.

Maybe it was the blueberry pancakes, but for some reason I couldn't stop thinking about my dad.

He'd worked as an editor and spent long hours locked up in his office, going over manuscripts. It was the first place I always checked when I came home from school or work. I hadn't been able to step foot in his office since he died.

Editing was the perfect job for my dad because he was a loner. I couldn't picture him in a suit doing the nine to five thing at a big company. A fitness fanatic, when he wasn't working, he was usually running several miles almost every day along his favorite jogging trails. With the exception of his famous blueberry pancakes, he avoided sugar like the plague. He worked hard to keep himself healthy, which made his death from a heart attack the ultimate irony.

With only an hour left before my shift started, I only had time for a quick shower before changing into fresh clothing. It was a slow day at work. Rob sent Devin to do a few odd jobs around the hotel, which left me alone at the front desk. I didn't see much of him until he came to relieve me for my lunch break.

Thankfully, he stayed at the front desk with me after I returned. I hated manning the front desk alone. Without him keeping me company, the minutes seemed to tick by slowly. I kept waiting for him to bring up our middle of the night conversation, but he didn't. Instead, we passed the time in between check-ins and check-outs talking about other things. Then, the hotel's computers crashed. Rob told us to take down people's information so we could send them a receipt in the mail after everything was up and running again.

After Rob disappeared back into his office, the lobby door swung open and a man walked in. He stood in front of the desk and handed me the key card to his room. I explained the situation to him, and he didn't react well.

Furrowing his brows he said, "You're kidding me, right?"

"No, sir," I replied, trying not to feel intimidated by the anger in his voice. "I'm sorry for the inconvenience."

"You're sorry?" he snapped. "Well, sorry isn't going to work for me. Let me speak to your manager."

I stood there for a second, not sure whether I should try and calm him down somehow or just go and get Rob.

"Are you deaf or something?" He raised his voice. "I said I wanted to speak to your manager."

I turned to head for Rob's office. Devin grabbed my arm and spun me back around. He glared at the man who had just spoken to me. "Apologize to her now."

I don't know who was more shocked; the guest who looked up from his phone after Devin made his demand, or me.

"I'm not apologizing to anyone."

"Devin," I whispered. Confrontation was something I avoided at all costs.

"Look at me," Devin ordered the man. He spoke slowly and quietly, but there was no mistaking the anger in his voice. "You *will* apologize for being impolite, and then you'll leave."

For a moment the man looked stunned, almost hypnotized. I thought for sure he'd demand to speak to Rob again and both Devin and I would get fired. Instead, he turned to me and said, "I'm sorry for being impolite." He even sounded contrite. "I need to leave."

I watched him walk away, still not sure exactly what had just happened and spooked by the way he repeated Devin's words.

When the door closed behind him, I looked at Devin. "What did you just do?"

"Nothing," he muttered.

"No, it wasn't nothing," I said. "How'd you get him to do that?"

"He had no business speaking to you like that, so I asked him politely to apologize and he complied."

"Uh, uh. No way." I had no idea how Devin made that man to apologize, but there was more to it than he let on. Somehow, I just knew it.

"What are you suggesting? That I have some sort of magical power and can make people do whatever I will them to? You told me yourself last night that you don't believe in magic."

I did say that. Because it was true. Still, I couldn't shake the feeling that Devin was keeping something from me. And this wasn't the first time, either.

After a pause, I said, "You know what I find curious? Why is it that you know so much about me, yet I hardly know about your life at all?"

"What is it you want to know?" he asked.

I wasn't sure how to respond. I didn't have any specific questions, but I felt a growing sense that Devin had secrets.

"Why Crescent City? Of all the places you could've moved to, why here?"

"I like the ocean, and the trees."

"And that's it? You're not some escaped gang-banger from Pelican Bay?"

He looked at me quizzically. "I don't know what either of those things are, so I'm pretty sure the answer is no."

I'd only been joking, but his response threw me. "How do you not know what Pelican Bay is? It's only the most notorious prison in the country and where, like, half of the people in Crescent City work."

"I knew that," Devin said, smiling. "I was just teasing."

He wasn't. I didn't need to be a mind reader to figure that out, but decided not to press the issue.

At just after five I signed out. Devin was busy checking someone in, so, instead of saying goodbye, I scribbled him a note. Halfway through the parking lot, he caught up with me.

"Where are you going?"

"Home."

"I can't convince you to come back to my house?"

As tempted as I was by the offer, I turned him down. I wasn't looking forward to going home to an empty house, but I couldn't put it off forever. The longer I did, the harder it would be.

"No." I shook my head. "It's not that I don't want to, it's just that . . . I really should go home."

"I'm going to worry about you, "Devin said. "I don't like the idea of you being on your own."

The concerned look on his face made me regret what I'd told him the night before. He was already protective when it came to me. What had I been thinking? Giving him one more thing to worry about had been a bad idea, but I couldn't take it back now.

"Yeah, well. One way or another, I'm going to have to get used to it."

"Why? Why do you have to get used to it when you can stay with me?"

"You wouldn't understand."

Devin reached for my hand. "Then make me understand."

"I can't."

He didn't get it and he never would. He'd never under-stand what it felt like to want someone in a different way than they wanted you. Normally, I managed to deal with it, but after I'd opened myself up to him, after I lay in his arms all night, it was harder than it had ever been before. With every day that passed, and every caring thing Devin did for me, it became more difficult to settle for just his friendship.

I pulled my hand away and turned to look for my car. I felt his eyes on me as I walked away, with each step half-hoping he'd try and stop me.

He didn't.

Chapter 7

AN EERIE SILENCE greeted me as I stepped inside the house Dad and I had shared. I regretted turning down Devin's invitation. Usually, when I got home, I called out a greeting to my father. Now, I caught myself before doing it, and a sinking feeling came over me. Grief felt like a bottomless pit. I would always feel Dad's absence. There were reminders of him everywhere. The distractions of the day—work, Devin—stopped the bleeding in my heart. Now, in the quiet solitude of home, the wound opened again.

I hated crying. Once I started, I felt like I couldn't stop. I bit my bottom lip and blinked back tears as I ran up the stairs to my bedroom.

Checking email and surfing the web helped occupy my thoughts most of the evening, but eventually my mind drifted. Thoughts of Devin crept in to my head between memories of Dad. At midnight I was still awake and tempted to take another sleeping pill, but fear of turning into a pill freak stopped me. Finally I drifted off to sleep on the couch with the TV on in the middle of another Law and Order rerun.

The next morning, I awoke to the sound of my doorbell ringing.

Still in pajamas, I pulled the door open to find my friend, Emma, standing on the threshold. I hadn't spoken to her since Dad's funeral.

"Emma, hi!" I said.

"Were you expecting someone else?" she joked as she stepped inside.

"No, but I wasn't expecting you, either. What are you doing here?" As the question left my mouth I realized it had been almost a month since we'd hung out. I felt bad that I'd let that happen.

She placed the two coffee cups she'd brought with her on the side table and flopped onto the couch.

"I have news, big news, and since you never answer your phone anymore, I decided to just show up." Her eyes scanned over my attire. "You were still in bed? Crap. I'm sorry."

"It's fine, don't worry about it." I took a seat next to her and reached for the coffee cup without the lipstick smear on it. "What's your big news?"

"Well, you already know Tim and I are going to UCLA, right?"

I nodded. How could I forget? It was all she talked about since she and her boyfriend had gotten accepted. UCLA was her one-way ticket out of dead-end Crescent City, and the fact that she was going with the love of her life made her doubly happy.

"Get this . . ." Emma practically bubbled over with excitement. "My mom said Tim and I can get a place together. Can you believe it? She's actually letting us move in with each other."

"Whoa!" Tim and Emma were tight; they had been for almost all of high school, but her news still came as a surprise. "Are you serious?"

"You don't think we should, do you? You think we're too young."

"I didn't say that. I'm just surprised, that's all."

"I know we're only eighteen, but I love Tim and he loves me, and I just know that there's no one else out there for me but him." It sounded like she was trying to convince me. I didn't need convincing, though. Emma and Tim were the two most right for each other people I'd ever met. They were both quirky in their own unique way. The only things Tim loved more than Emma were gadgets—computers, video games, smartphones, you name it. Emma didn't mind his obsession. She saw him as a genius, which he was. And anyone who knew Tim could tell he thought he was the luckiest guy on the planet to have a girlfriend as smart and cute as Emma, a girl who actually found his nerdiness appealing.

"I'm so happy for you." I hugged her. "So when are you guys leaving for LA?"

"Oh yeah, you just reminded me, that's the other thing I wanted to tell you. Classes don't start until September, but Tim and I are leaving in a few weeks so we can look around for an apartment and get to know the city first."

"A few weeks?" Emma and I hadn't seen much of each other since graduation, but the idea that she and Tim would be gone so soon bothered me. I didn't like that I was losing two more people that I cared about.

"Tim's dad is throwing us a goodbye party next Friday. Can you come?"

"Next Friday? Yeah, I can come. I'm off Friday, and the day after, too."

"You can bring Devin if you want," she said. "How is he anyway?"

I was still processing Emma's news and almost didn't hear her question. "He's fine."

"And what about you? I was so busy telling you about me and Tim that I didn't think to ask . . ."

"Don't worry about it. I'm doing all right." I knew what Emma was about to say. I looked around the living room. A framed picture of me and my dad stood on the side table next to the couch. Neither Katy nor I had touched any of his things since he died. "I miss Dad like crazy, but every day it's a little easier."

"There are so many memories here," Emma said.

"Devin asked me to move in with him." I had no idea what compelled me to share that bit of news. Maybe I didn't want a walk down memory lane, or maybe it was her announcement that she and Tim were getting an apartment together, although their situation was completely different.

"Wait a minute . . . I thought you guys were just friends."

"We are." I shrugged. "He only asked because he's worried about me living here alone."

"He's got a point. You know Crescent City is filled with meth heads. Getting a roommate isn't a bad idea. But . . . I'm not sure about Devin, you know, because of the way you feel about him and all."

My head snapped up. "Wait a minute. I never told you I liked Devin."

"It doesn't take a genius to figure it out, Lilli."

My shoulders slumped. "Do you think he knows?"

"I have no idea. I've only talked to him a few times. But every time I did I kind of got the feeling that he liked you right back." She took a sip of her coffee. "You know guys these days like girls who make the first move; maybe *you* should ask him out."

I shook my head. "No way."

*

I spent the rest of the day thinking about what Emma had said. There wasn't a way in the world I was going to ask Devin on a date, but I wondered if she was right about him liking me back. Maybe he thought I didn't share his feelings, or that it was too soon after my dad died to bring it up. Whatever the reason, Devin held himself back, and I had no idea what to do about it.

When he called later in the day to say hi, I thought about what Emma had said. Even though I'd sworn that there was no way I was going to ask him out on a date, inviting him to a party was totally within the realm of friendship.

"You remember my friend Emma?" I asked him.

"Kind of short, reddish hair, blue eyes?"

"Yeah, that's the one."

"What about her?"

"She invited me to a party at her boyfriend Tim's house. It's next Friday. Do you want to come?"

"A party?" Devin sounded unsure.

"Not a big one." Like me, he wasn't a fan of crowds. "It's probably just going to be handful of kids from our school."

I waited for Devin to reply, thinking maybe I should say, "Don't worry about it," before he had a chance to turn me down. I'd never been what anyone would call a social butterfly. But if I was bad about keeping to myself too often, Devin was worse. In some ways, it felt like he dropped into my life out of nowhere, as if he was in Crescent City for me. As crazy and stupid as it sounded, the thought warmed me. He seemed to have little interest in making an army of friends the way most other people did—yet another thing about him I found odd, but at the same time really liked.

"You don't have to come if you don't want to."

"Wait a minute. I didn't say I don't want to go. It sounds like fun, actually. I was just wondering what one wears to a party in Crescent City?"

I laughed. "You act like Crescent City is in another world. We wear the same things here that everyone else does."

"Right. So jeans and a t-shirt then?"

"Yes. Jeans and a t-shirt are perfect."

My dad noticed it about Devin first—the way he seemed to not know certain things most other people did. Like when I made the joke about Pelican Bay prison, or the time he gave my dad a clueless look when asked whether he'd taken the SAT or ACT. Devin explained it away by telling us that he grew up in a small town. He didn't go to school; his parents taught him at home. He didn't use the word home-schooled, though, or other common expressions most people did. His parents didn't believe in television or the Internet. I figured it was his upbringing that caused him not to see himself the way most other people did. It also explained why he wasn't always sure about things I considered common knowledge, like what you wear to a party at a friend's house.

"Okay, well, I guess I'll see you at work tomorrow?"

"Yeah. I'll be there."

"Before you hang up, I need you to do me a favor."

"What's that?"

"Can you make sure you lock your door . . . and your windows, too?"

"This is Crescent City," I said, with a groan. "Not New York City. You worry too much."

"If something were to happen to you, I'd never forgive myself, and since you refused my offer to move in together, you will just have to put up with me pestering you."

I smiled, inwardly grateful for his pestering, enjoying the way it made me imagine that there had to be a reason he cared so much. "Good night, Devin."

*

The day of Emma and Tim's party eventually came. Devin, at work without me, called early in the morning.

"What time are you picking me up again?" he asked.

"Around six."

"Oh." A long pause followed. "What are you doing until then?"

"Just running errands, I guess."

"Alone?" He didn't sound happy about it.

"Yeah, why not?"

"Uh . . . no reason." He paused. "I guess I'll see you later then."

Things had been weird between us ever since I'd spent the night at his house. He was protective before, but now he treated me like I was made of glass, fragile and easy to break. I tried to goad him into explaining why he was so protective, but all he ever said was that he didn't like the idea of me being by myself—not exactly the answer I was hoping for. I imagined him telling me instead that he was madly in love with me and couldn't stand the idea of anything bad happening to me. It brought a smile to my face, but eventually I snapped back to reality.

I filled my day vacuuming, grocery shopping, and doing laundry. I tried not to think about Devin. By the time I pulled up in front of his house later, I'd almost convinced myself that just being friends was fine with me. When he stepped out of his house and climbed into the passenger seat of my car, my resolve shattered.

Chapter 8

MY EYES WANDERED over Devin as I took in his appearance. He wore all black, which brought out the color of his eyes. His shirt clung to his torso, accentuating his broad shoulders and chest. He'd combed his still wet wavy hair back off his forehead. I stared at him without meaning to and only turned my head to avert his gaze when I realized what I was doing. If I looked into his eyes a second longer, I would drown in them.

"So what do you think? Do I look all right?"

I refused to turn my head in his direction again. Instead, I swallowed the lump in my throat. He looked more than all right.

"Yeah," I said quickly. "You look fine."

We made it to Tim's house a few minutes later. I got out of the car, and even though it was chilly outside I took my jacket off, balled it up and threw it in the backseat. I didn't feel like carrying it with me all night.

Devin's eyes locked on me.

"Is something wrong?" I said.

"No. You look beautiful, but maybe it's too cold to leave your jacket behind."

I looked down at the shirt I'd chosen earlier. A gift from Katy, dark brown and silky, the tank top fell a little lower than shirts I normally wore. I paired it with jeans and sandals. Usually I didn't wear makeup, but tonight I'd put on some sparkly eye shadow and lip-gloss.

"Thank you," I said, regretting that it wasn't yet dark enough to hide the blush that I could feel creeping into my cheeks, but happy that Devin liked the way I looked. "But I think I'll be fine without it."

Music blared from inside Tim's house. I rang the bell a few times, then knocked loudly. When nobody answered, I let us in. The crowd and loud music made me instantly nervous. When Emma had invited me, I'd expected a small gathering of our classmates. If I'd known there were going to be so many strangers, I would've turned down her invitation, or at least mentally prepared myself for the chance of having one of my bizarre visions.

The smell of barbecue wafted into the house through the patio door, which opened as someone walked in with a plate of food. I moved through the house, pulling Devin behind me toward the backyard, trying to avoid making eye contact, but at the same time trying to find Tim or Emma. Just as we stepped out onto the patio, I felt a tap on my arm and heard Tim's familiar voice greeting me.

"Who are all these people?" I asked.

He rolled his eyes. "My dad decided to invite my cousin from Santa Cruz, and he came with a bunch of his friends. I don't even know most of them."

"Isn't this supposed to be your party?" I shouted over the music.

"It was. I didn't really want a party, but my dad insisted."

As long as I'd known Tim, his dad was always trying to get him to be someone he wasn't. When we were kids, he endured spring after spring of Little League until his father finally gave in and realized that his son and sports were not meant to be. That was probably one of the reasons Tim decided on a school so far away, not just to get away from Crescent City, but to get away from his dad.

"Who's your friend?" Tim asked. I'd almost forgotten that he and Devin had never met.

I finished the introductions just as Emma came over. She gave me a hug and grabbed Devin's hand. "C'mon, let me show you where the food is," she said, pulling him away. I turned my attention back to Tim just as one of our former classmates, Allison, sidled up next to him.

"Who *is* that guy?" Allison asked me.

It took me a moment to realize she was referring to Devin. "A friend of mine. We work together at the Tides."

"Oh my God, he's so cute. Can you introduce us?" Without giving me a chance to answer, she continued. "You know what? Forget it, I'll do it myself." She took off, apparently to look for Devin. I fought the temptation to chase after her, telling myself that if Devin was interested in someone like her, then he wasn't the person I thought he was, after all.

Meeting Allison at Tim and Emma's party surprised me. Neither of them hung out with her at school. More than once, Allison referred to them as the nerd crew, and I was pretty sure they knew. Although that was better than the nickname she'd given me in junior high—Mrs. Creepy.

Before I could disengage from Tim, his father interrupted. The smell of alcohol on his breath just about knocked me sideways. I craned my neck in search of Devin as Tim's dad talked my ear off about how he was going to miss his boy.

"Hey, Uncle Greg!" A boy I'd never seen before slung his arm around Tim's father's shoulder. Looking at me, he said, "Who's this?"

"Tim's friend from school. Her name's Lilli—and she's single." He actually winked as the words left his mouth.

The boy held out his hand. "Hi, I'm Tim's cousin, Carson."

I felt like taking a swing at Tim's dad instead of shaking hands. I'd almost forgotten how much pleasure the man derived from embarrassing people.

Carson looked a bit older than Tim. His tall, lanky frame was topped with longish blond hair that swept down over his forehead, brushing the tops of his eyes, in a hipster surferboy style.

"So you're Tim's cousin?" I said as Tim's dad went to go find someone else to humiliate.

"Yup, that's me." He reached behind his back for a beer from the patio table and tried to hand it to me.

"Um . . . I'm only eighteen," I stammered.

"This is a party, isn't it? Who's gonna tell?"

"No thanks." I didn't want to be a prude, but I wasn't interested in drinking. Seeing Tim's dad tipsy was kind of sobering and, besides, the one time I'd tried beer, I hadn't liked the taste.

"Suit yourself." He opened the bottle and chugged half of it down. "Tim never told me they had such pretty girls up here in Crescent City. I wonder why he's been holding back on me. The two of you don't have anything going on, do you?"

"You do know that he has a girlfriend?" I said, realizing that this was the other reason I hated parties. Drinking and loud music seemed to bring out the worst in people.

"Oh yeah, that's right."

I looked around, hoping to find an excuse to slip away. Thankfully, I spotted Devin approaching and hoped he would succeed in easing me away from Carson's unwelcome company.

When Devin reached us he put his arm around my waist and glared at Carson. "Go away," he said, his voice a low rumble. There was no mistaking the anger in it.

"*What* did you just say?" Carson asked indignantly as he squared his shoulders.

For a second, I thought the two of them would get into it. I desperately tried to think of something to say to diffuse the situation.

"I. Said. Go. Away."

Devin pronounced each word slowly and sternly. When the last word rolled off his tongue, to my utter amazement, Carson stared at me for a second, then Devin, and without a word turned on his heel and did as Devin commanded, like a dog obeying its master. Just a few minutes ago, Carson had come across as pretty sure of himself, I wondered why he allowed Devin to speak to him like that.

"What just happened?" I asked.

"What are you talking about?" Devin grumbled, looking past me like he wasn't interested in conversation.

"You know what I'm talking about," I stammered. "How did you get him to do that?"

"Why? Did you want him to keep ogling you? Were you

hoping for more time with him?" Devin's voice was still laced with anger.

"No, of course not! But—" I wasn't really sure what to say. It wasn't the first time I'd seen Devin do that. I told him that I didn't believe he had magical powers, but I was seriously beginning to question whether I might've been wrong. Before I could think of anything to say, he grabbed me by my arm and headed back inside the house, pulling me along with him.

"Can we go?" he said. "I'm not feeling comfortable here."

"Um . . . okay. Let me say bye to Tim and Emma first," I replied. Truthfully, I'd wanted to leave less than a minute after I stepped through the door.

Emma spotted me walking toward her. She ran up brimming with excitement. "Oh my God, Lilli. Devin is sooo into you."

"What are you talking about?"

"You should've seen him when you were talking to Carson. It looked like he wanted to rip his head off."

"I think you're exaggerating just a bit." Devin was upset about something, that much I'd figured out, but jealousy over a stupid conversation, it didn't seem possible. Besides, the music was too loud for him to have heard a word Carson had said to me.

"He looks even hotter tonight than he usually does," Emma said dreamily. I wondered if she'd been drinking, too. "I bet he's a good kisser, did you see his lips?"

"Of course I've seen them. I work with him practically every day."

"I don't know how you stand it."

"Don't you have a boyfriend, one that you're about to move in with?"

"That doesn't mean I don't have eyes anymore."

"I was looking for you so I could say bye." *Not talk about how hot Devin is.* Hearing her gush about him irked me. I felt territorial about him. Since when had I come to think of him as mine?

"Why are you leaving so soon?"

"Just tired," I replied.

I gave her a quick hug and wished her well. She promised to tell Tim bye for me, and then I escaped to find Devin.

He was waiting by my car with a stormy expression on his face. I slid into the driver's seat, and as I drove away, I tried to figure out why he seemed so upset. I had no clue what had set him off. I'd thought the party would be fun for him. We'd been at Tim's for less than half an hour, and he gave me the impression that he wasn't remotely interested in being there. Why had he agreed to come in the first place?

"What's wrong?" I finally asked.

"Nothing, it's stupid," he muttered.

I wasn't used to this version of Devin. Overprotective Devin I could get used to, but unexplained mood shifts were harder. "What is?"

He shifted in his seat and turned his body towards mine. "Have you ever wanted something you had no right to have?" he asked.

There were plenty of things I wanted, but I never thought about whether or not I had the right to have them. "There's nothing wrong with wanting," I said.

"Yes. Yes there is." He answered with torment in his voice. It made me sad for him.

"Tell me what's going on." I waited for him to reply, but the car remained filled with a heavy silence as I drove. "I've trusted you with my deepest secrets. Why can't you trust me with yours?"

"Because I'm afraid," Devin said, as I pulled into his driveway.

"When I told you about my dreams and about my mother I was, too, but I trusted you anyway." I parked and waited for him to say something, but we just sat there.

"Walk me to my door?" he finally said.

"Sure." We both got out of the car, Devin waited for me as I made my way to the passenger's side where he stood. He reached for one of my hands and pulled me toward him. The two of us stood just stood there facing each other. After what seemed like forever he took my other hand in his.

"I'm sorry if I ruined your night," he said.

"You didn't. I'm not really into parties anyway."

"Can you come inside and stay the night like you did before? I don't like being away from you."

"And why is that?" I managed to ask despite the pounding in my chest.

He sighed and leaned towards me, his forehead closing the space between us to rest on mine. I felt the contact like a jolt through my body.

"You know why," Devin whispered. "You have to know why. I've been trying to hide it, but I can't anymore."

"Hide what?"

"This," he said. His hands let go of mine and moved up to grasp the sides of my face.

A moment later he pulled me against him and then his lips were on mine. I melted into him, trembling. I hadn't expected a kiss, I'd just been hoping for words. Fireworks exploded inside me as his tongue parted my lips. The taste of him made my knees weak, but he held me tight and kept kissing me. I kissed him back and wrapped my arms around him. For months I'd day-dreamed about this moment, but the real thing was a million times better than my imagination. I felt like I could have stood in the driveway kissing him all night, but he pulled away. A look of horror crossed his face.

"I'm sorry, Lilli," he said, stepping away. "Please, don't be angry. I don't know what came over me."

"Why are you sorry?" I asked, confused. "And why would I be angry?"

"For taking advantage of you."

"You didn't take advantage of me. In case you didn't notice, I kissed you back." I took a step toward him and reached out to touch his arm.

He took my hand and lifted it up to his lips kissing it gently. "I don't deserve you."

"Why are you saying that?"

"Because it's true, Lilli. I wish it weren't, but it is."

"But you're not telling me why."

He lowered his gaze and shook his head. "Because after I tell you, I'll lose you for good."

"You won't lose me—that's crazy." I could tell I wasn't convincing him of anything.

"I have to go," he said. Before I could stop him, he turned away and ran inside his house without looking back, leaving me standing alone in his driveway, feeling utterly confused.

I racked my brain on the way home, trying to figure out what it was he couldn't tell me, but I came up empty. I contemplated at least a dozen possible scenarios, but none of them seemed right. All I knew, finally and for sure, was that he had feelings for me. I was tempted to drive back to his house and tell him I didn't care about his secrets, but the truth was I did care.

By the time I parked in my driveway, I was thoroughly exasperated. My phone rang just as I put my key in the door. Relieved to see Devin's number, I picked it up.

"Did you get home safely?" he asked.

"Yeah, I just pulled into the driveway."

"Good."

"Can we talk about what just happened?" I asked.

"We will, but not tonight. It has to be in person." He paused. "Are you inside your house yet?"

"I just locked the door behind me."

"Good. I have to go," he said. And then he hung up.

Chapter 9

HALF A DOZEN times that night I fought the temptation to pick up the phone and call Devin. I thought about our kiss and wondered how I could kiss someone, only to have them regret it and run in the opposite direction.

When I was done obsessing over our kiss, I agonized over what it was Devin needed to tell me. For months, I'd suspected there was something he wasn't telling me, but what could be that bad that he thought he had no right to me?

When I finally fell asleep, it wasn't for long. I woke up shaking from the same nightmare I'd had at Devin's house, except this time he wasn't there to wake me up, so the dream played out longer. The sound of the woman and her child crying must've alerted the people inside the building. A stream of cloaked figures ran out into the courtyard. They gathered around the woman who was holding her child in one arm and clutching her dead husband's hand with the other. Nothing they said consoled her. Eventually, one of them lifted the little boy into his arms and another carried the woman until they all disappeared back inside. The cries continued. I looked around trying to figure out where the noise was coming from.

Out of the corner of my eye, I spotted movement. I fixed my gaze on the statues that flanked the courtyard. They were somehow alive. Although they still looked stone, they were moving. One let out a roar, the other let its shoulders slump and head bow. Actual tears fell from their eyes. But how could statues cry? I woke up with the sound of their weeping still ringing in my ears. So much pain. I could hardly bear it. But why? I didn't know those people, they weren't even real, just figments of my overactive imagination. So why did they affect me the way they did?

When morning came, I tried to push thoughts of Devin out of my head, but eventually I couldn't stand it anymore and dialed his number. He didn't answer. I stared out of my kitchen window into the backyard, trying to decide how to spend my day off. I thought about going through my father's things. It was something I needed to do at some point, but I couldn't bring myself to go upstairs and open the door to his bedroom. Instead, I lay around all day alternating between watching TV and reading. By nightfall Devin still hadn't called and I went to bed, angry. I worried that things would be awkward at work the next day, but despite that, when morning came, I couldn't get to the hotel early enough.

Devin wasn't there when I walked through the lobby doors. I tried calling him, but my call went straight to voice-mail. A few minutes into my shift, Rob told me that Devin had called in sick. Maybe he believed Devin really was sick, but I wasn't buying it. I'd seen him two days before and he was totally fine. I dug my phone out of my pocket and called him again, ready to demand an explanation, but he didn't answer. Frustrated, I jammed my phone into the back pocket of my pants. If I was at home, instead of at work, I would have flung it against the wall.

"Excuse me, miss." A woman's voice broke through, interrupting my thoughts. I reminded myself that I was at work and turned to see what the person wanted.

"How can I help you?" I asked.

"I called for a few more towels over an hour ago," she said.

"I'm sorry." I gave her a half-hearted smile. "We'll have someone bring them over right away. What's your room number?" I jotted it down and she walked away.

The day dragged on, and the moment five o'clock rolled around I bolted out the door and headed straight for Devin's house. It was stupid, I knew it. He might not even be home and, even if he was, what would I say? And how would he respond? If he told me that kissing me was a mistake, I would die. It was foolish to have started something with him when my heart was still raw with the pain of losing my dad, but he was the one who kissed me, not the other way around.

I got to his house and spotted his car in the driveway. As I parked, he opened the door and stepped out to greet me, looking like he hadn't slept in days.

"You really are sick," I said. "Why didn't you call me?"

"I'm not sick. I've just had a lot on my mind."

"Are you going to invite me in?" I asked.

"Of course," he said, backing up to give me space to enter.

I turned around to face him as he closed the door. "Are you going to tell me what the hell is going on or are you going to keep me guessing?" I demanded. My stomach twisted into a knot. "Because if you're not really interested in me, then you should just say so." I hadn't intended to blurt everything out like that, but now that I had, there was no taking it back.

He looked surprised, then confused. "No, you got it all wrong, Lilli," he said, shaking his head. "The truth is, I've never felt for anyone the way I do for you."

His confession took me by surprise. I desperately wanted to believe it, but, if it was true, why had he been avoiding me for the past two days? "Then what's the problem?"

"We should sit." Devin and I settled down on the couch beside each other. He turned to face me. "I'm glad you came over. I shouldn't have missed work today; it was stupid of me. It's just that—I needed some time to think."

"About?"

"About the right words to use."

"What do you mean the right words?" All of a sudden I felt sick to my stomach, afraid that he was going to say that we could only be friends.

"I want to tell you everything. Every secret, every single thing I know that you don't. The problem is I want to tell you for all the wrong reasons, and I hate myself for it."

"You've lost me."

His beautiful eyes looked conflicted. I wanted to fix whatever was hurting him, just like he always tried to fix things for me.

"The right thing to do is walk away and go back to where I came from, so you can have the life you were supposed to. The problem is, I don't know how to do that."

He was talking in circles, confusing me instead of clearing things up. "What kind of life am I supposed to have?"

Devin looked straight in to my eyes before answering, "The life your mother wanted you to have."

Chapter 10

A BARRAGE OF QUESTIONS flooded my mind and I tried to sort through them and decide which one I needed answered first. "How would you know what kind of life my mother wanted for me?"

"How do I put this?" Devin paused, searching for the right words. "Since I've gotten to know you, I've been able to put a few things together."

Another vague reply. Something he was frustratingly good at. "You have to stop giving me half-answers. Whatever it is you need to say, just spit it out already."

Devin took a deep breath. "You asked me more than once what brought me to Crescent City, and I told you it was the ocean and the trees. Do you remember that?" I nodded, and he continued. "What you should have asked is what made me stay."

"Okay," I said, hoping we were finally getting somewhere. "Tell me. Why did you decide to stay in Crescent City?"

"I stayed because of you."

"Me? Why?"

"It's—well." Devin began to fidget, opening and closing

his hands and then staring at them like they had the answers he was looking for. "I've felt like an outcast for as long as I can remember. I think, because of that, I've always wondered what life was like away from home. So one day I decided to find out."

"And that's how you wound up in Crescent City?"

"Yes. Although it wasn't the first place I visited. In fact, I had every intention of moving on and continuing my travels until I saw you."

"At the coffee shop?"

Devin shook his head. "That wasn't the first time I saw you. The first time was weeks before that. I'm sure you thought of our meeting as pure coincidence, that I happened to stumble upon you just as you were searching for a job, but that's not true. I'd been following you around for a while, trying to think of a way to get to know you, and that day in the coffee shop a chance presented itself."

"Why would you want to get to know me?" Maybe the idea of Devin following me around should've freaked me out, but I was too focused on trying to make sense of what he was telling me.

"I wanted to know why you were here in Crescent City instead of with your mother."

His answer stunned me. "What?!"

"You look just like her," Devin continued, oblivious to my outburst. "You have Naiara's eyes, her hair, and her fair skin. From a distance, I actually thought you were her. Then I realized that wasn't right, but you look too much like her to be anything but her daughter."

My head spun. Somehow Devin had known my mother? But that wasn't possible. He was only a year and a half older than me. She died when I was a few months old, and he, too would've been too young to remember her.

"How do you know I look like her?" I'd talked to him about my mother, plenty of times, but I hadn't told him that. Maybe he'd just assumed.

"I've known your mother my whole life."

"That's impossible," I said, feeling an odd sense of frustration brewing inside me. "She's dead, and has been for a long time."

"No." He shook his head. "She's not."

"Devin, why are you doing this?" He had to know how painful this was, especially after everything I'd confided in him.

"I don't want to hurt you, but I owe you the truth."

"Just . . . whatever this is all about, can you spit it out already?"

Devin sighed and rested his hands on his knees as if he were bracing himself. "Like I said, I've known your mother for as long as I can remember." He turned his head toward me. "You believe she's dead, but she's not. When I came to Crescent City and saw you, I knew you were her child. What I didn't know was why you were here without her. It made me curious and I wanted answers, so I followed you, hoping to find out, but what I discovered only led to more questions. I realized the only way to figure out what you were doing here was to get to know you, to become your friend, and helping you find a job seemed like a good way to do that."

I stared at him, eyes wide with disbelief. A part of me wanted to believe he was right, that my mother was alive, but I just couldn't bring myself to. Still, I didn't think he was lying. He believed every word he was telling me, which meant he'd had an ulterior motive for being my friend and had been keeping me in the dark about it for months. "And . . . did you get all your questions answered?" I choked out.

"I think so. There are, of course, missing pieces of information, but your mother is the one who has those."

"Right, of course."

Devin ignored the sarcasm in my voice and continued. "The best I can figure is that your mother must have come here to Crescent City at some point and fallen in love with your father. But Naiara was promised to someone else already. Perhaps she realized the man who thought of her as his would hunt her down, and that he'd find her here with another man *and* his child. She must have left to protect the two of you."

"Who is this him you keep referring to?" I asked, intrigued by Devin's story. Even though I remained skeptical, the voice inside my head that kept telling me he knew too many things I hadn't shared—like my mother's name and how I looked so much like her—got louder by the second.

"Your mother's husband. Zoran is his name."

"My mother is married?" My stomach tightened at the idea of her with someone else after I'd spent my entire life watching what her absence had done to my father.

"Yes," Devin replied.

"Was she married to him when she met my dad?"

"Not technically. But they were promised to each other from childhood, which means they've belonged to each other since then and no one else."

By promised to each other, I figured Devin meant engaged. I tried sifting through all the information he had just given me. My mind was a jumbled mess. His whole story was insane. I took a deep breath. "Let me see if I'm getting this straight. My mother left the man she was supposed to marry, met my dad and fell in love with him, then gave birth to me and left us just in case her fiancée found out?"

"Yes. I suppose that's as good an explanation as any."

I clenched my hands into fists and felt my fingernails leave little half-moon welts in my palms. Why would Devin tell me something so outlandish?

"You do realize this story makes no sense, right? If she was afraid, she could have called the police, got an order of protection or something. She's been gone for almost eighteen years. You're telling me in that whole time she couldn't have called my dad even once to let him know what happened to her?"

"It's not that simple. Where your mother and I are from, things don't really work the way they do here. We don't have police, and since I'm not certain what an order of protection is, I'm pretty sure we don't have those, either."

"What are you talking about? Where exactly are you from?"

"We're from . . ." He paused before answering. "Our home is called the Wilds."

"The Wilds? Where's that?"

"You can't find it on any map, Lilli. At least not on any human map."

I frowned. "And why is that?"

Trying to find the right words, he glanced at me, then fixed his gaze on his hands, which he held in his lap, fingers laced tightly together. "The Wilds isn't part of this world. It's a place humans can't get to, a place of magic."

"Magic?"

Devin's serious expression threw me. It seemed impossible that he actually believed what he was saying. No wonder he didn't think I was crazy after I told him about my dreams—because he was completely and totally out of his mind. All I could do was stare at him, speechless.

"You don't believe me," he finally said, offended.

"Oh, come on, Devin. You didn't really think I would, did you?" I laid my hand gently on his shoulder. "But you're completely sure that *you* believe it?" I wanted to give him a chance to back out, save his dignity.

"Yes, of course." His lips curled into a mad grin. "Why would you believe me?" he asked rhetorically.

"Devin, why are you doing this?"

"I finally work up the courage to tell you the truth, knowing what it could cost me, and you don't believe me."

There was nothing to say, but I tried anyway. "You know I care about you . . ."

He started to laugh. "You think I'm crazy, don't you? You *actually* think I'm crazy." He looked at me waiting for a denial, but I couldn't give it to him. "Fine, since you don't believe me, then I guess I'll just have to show you."

"Show me what?"

"The truth."

Chapter 11

I SIGHED AND FOLDED my arms across my chest, not sure what else to say. Devin got up from the couch and took a few steps. Then, before my eyes, he disappeared. I gasped. *Breathe, Lilli.* If I hadn't been sitting down, my legs would have given out from under me. I felt faint and nauseous and convinced that I was losing my mind, *again.* Just like I had at my father's funeral.

I reached out towards the spot Devin had just been standing in, but he'd vanished, just like my mother had at Dad's funeral. I'd convinced myself that I'd seen her ghost. Devin certainly wasn't one of those, which meant there had to be another explanation.

"Lilli."

I turned. Devin's voice came from the hallway that led to his room. I got up to follow it and saw him as he walked down the hall towards me.

"What the hell?" I said as I wrapped my arms around myself, protectively. "How did you do that?"

"Magic."

"What?" I looked up at him, still not certain that my

mind wasn't playing tricks on me. I backed away as he approached me.

"Let's sit back down."

I hesitated for a moment, but, realizing that I needed him to explain things, I took a seat beside him and waited for him to start talking. "It's called magic, Lilli. That's how I can teleport."

"Magic?" I'd spent most of my life trying to convince myself that there was no such thing, and here Devin was, telling me I was wrong, and at the same time showing me I wasn't crazy. It should've been a relief, but maybe thinking myself insane was better than realizing so much of my life had been a lie. "What are you saying, that you're some sort of magician?"

"Well, I suppose that is one of the terms used to describe our kind . . ."

"Our kind?"

"Witches, Lilli. You, me, your mother, that's what we are; the sons and daughters of magic."

"Witches?" I waited for him to say he was joking, but he didn't. I knew there were people who *thought* they had powers, who worshipped the occult, but I'd never been into that sort of thing. "Oh, come on. I am *not* a witch, I don't believe in that stuff."

"Being a witch is not something you get to decide to be. Whatever you think you may know from what you've seen on TV or read in some human book, get it out of your head. Being a witch is in your blood, it's who you are. And despite our appearance, we are no more human than elves or fairies."

"It can't be," I whispered.

I tried to turn my head away. Devin reached for my chin

and forced me to meet his gaze. "This doesn't have to change anything between us, Lilli."

"Devin, I don't believe in witches and magic."

He looked at me as if he couldn't understand my refusal to accept everything he'd just told me. "You still don't, even after what I showed you?"

It wasn't that I didn't believe him. It was that I didn't *want* to believe him. Not like I had any other choice. Whatever he'd just done couldn't be explained away.

"I don't have any powers. I can't do what you just did," I said, hoping that Devin would take it all back about me being a witch. Ever since I'd started having my strange dreams and seeing monsters, all I wanted was a normal life, and I still did. I wanted a mother and father who were still alive, a brother or sister and a handful of cousins, too. I wanted to leave Crescent City and go to college. I didn't want anything he'd just told me to be true. Then I flashed back to the last few dreams I'd had about the monsters killing that man in the courtyard. They'd referred to the man and his family as witches. I couldn't shake the feeling that I had that dream for a reason.

"There are all sorts of reasons for that, I imagine." Devin scooted closer to me and took my hands in his. "You haven't had anyone to teach you about magic and you're technically only a half-witch, since your father wasn't one. I suppose that's one explanation."

"And the other?"

"I'm afraid your mother is the only one who can answer that question, and there isn't any way for me to reach her from here."

"Why is that?"

"It's a bit hard to explain, but I'll try my best," Devin said. He let go of my hands. "Picture the world as one of those interrogation rooms the police on TV use when they're questioning someone. On one side are the people you've lived with your entire life: mortals, regular humans with no magical abilities. They're the ones in the room with the window you can't see through. We're on the other side of that glass. Witches, fairies, demons and all things magical that you've probably read about but always assumed were make-believe. We can see through the glass, even though whoever is behind it can't see us. We know what exists beyond our part of the world, but humans have no idea what exists outside of theirs. We are in two different worlds. If I wanted to speak to Naiara, I'd have to return to the Wilds."

"How is any of this even possible?" I shook my head. "If I'm really a witch, why don't I know about anything you just explained?"

"You do. You just don't realize it. At your father's funeral, you and I were the only ones who could see your mother. Magical beings use glamour to hide themselves when they travel through human lands and want to remain unseen. Only another magical being can see them, like you did. And the dreams you've been having, they're of us. You said it yourself, you dream about witches and magic all the time. Now you know why."

Glamour. I knew what that was from the pile of books I'd read about fairies and vampires. It was magic used to hide the true form of a person. I pulled away. Leaning back against the couch cushions, I closed my eyes, and tried to process everything Devin had just told me. Conflicting thoughts tumbled through my mind. Not only had Devin been lying to me for months and keeping secrets, but the only reason he had befriended me was to satisfy his curiosity. For months I'd been convinced the two of us were at least friends, if not something more, but if it weren't for Devin's ulterior motives the two of us would never have met, never became friends—never kissed. How much of what we shared was real and how much of it was a trick to get me to open up?

"What are you thinking, Lilli?" Devin said.

I opened my eyes and turned to look at him. He still had his hands clenched in his lap. "That you're a liar and a user."

"I swear it's not like that, Lilli," Devin said, his voice pleading. "I wanted to tell you the truth for a long time; I just didn't know how."

"*That* is not an excuse." I wavered between anger and a deep ache that tore at my insides. Tears sprang from my eyes and I wiped them away before they could start rolling down my face. I had trusted Devin. I let him in and told him my deepest darkest secrets because I thought he cared for me. There were a million words that needed to come out, but none of them were able to make it to the surface. "I need to get out of here," I finally said. I stood, grabbed my bag, and headed towards the door.

"Lilli, we have to talk about this," Devin pleaded as I grabbed the doorknob, ready to make my escape. "You can't just push me away."

"Yes. I can." I shook my head and wrapped my arms around myself again. "I don't want to hear anymore. I just want to be alone."

I threw the door open and ran outside. Devin followed me. I got inside my car and locked the doors. He knocked on the window, but I refused to lower it.

"This isn't over, Lilli. Even if you don't want to have anything else to do with me, there are more things I have to tell you. Things you need to know."

I turned the engine on, put my car in drive, and pulled away from the curb, but not before I heard him say, "Lilli, please, your life could be in danger."

Chapter 12

EVERYTHING DEVIN HAD told me seemed impossible. If I hadn't seen him teleport in front of my eyes, I wouldn't have believed a word of it. I didn't want to believe it. I wanted things to go back to the way they were before. Back to that night when he kissed me for the first time and I felt like the luckiest girl alive.

I raced through the streets on my way home, struggling against the desire to turn around, because as angry as I was with Devin, I still wanted him. I still *needed* him.

When I got home, I stormed inside and slammed the door shut. I wasn't sure what to do. Nothing became clearer as I sat on the couch, trying to sort things out in my mind, but the longer I sat doing nothing, the more frustrated I became. I climbed the stairs and burst into my bedroom. I pulled open my nightstand drawer and stared at my mother's picture, tempted to rip it to shreds. She'd been alive this whole time. A few weeks ago she'd been standing only a few feet away from me, but instead of talking to me, she'd used her magic to disappear, not bothering to consider what that would do to me. For so long my heart had ached for her, but now I felt something different. Anger. Betrayal.

A long shower helped calm me down, but as soon as I dried myself off, my mind started racing again. When I was done in the bathroom, I sat down at my desk, opened my laptop and typed the word "witch" in the search engine, even though I knew the Internet would just give me a bunch of bogus information. I tried searching for the Wilds next, the place Devin said he was from. Google seemed to think it was some safari park in Ohio, which obviously wasn't the same place Devin referred to earlier.

Over the years, I'd read a whole stack of books with stories that took place in pretend worlds, and I still remembered most of their settings; Narnia, Avalon, Middle Earth. But those were stories, fantasy. I tried to imagine what my mother's life in the Wilds was like. Maybe it was so amazing that she forgot all about the people she'd left behind.

As I lay in bed that night trying to sleep, I decided it didn't matter that I was a half-witch. I had no real powers, and a part of me began to feel relieved that I wasn't crazy after all. Seeing my mother, having crazy dreams about magic and people dying—there was a reason those things happened. I didn't like the reason, but at least there was one.

Everything will be all right, I tried telling myself.

In the morning, after getting out of bed, I wasn't so sure. It suddenly dawned on me that the chances were close to zero that I'd ever see my mother again. She was stuck in her part of the world and it looked like I was stuck in mine. I couldn't help but feel sad that I'd probably never get to meet her, much less get a chance to know her.

Too angry and hurt to face Devin, I decided to call in

sick to work before texting Emma and convincing her to come hang out with me. We decided to meet downtown for lunch. My phone rang every fifteen minutes as I got ready to leave the house, but I let the calls go to voicemail. I couldn't avoid Devin forever, but I wasn't ready to face him yet. Did he think I had more secrets to share? Was the kiss just a part of his plan to get close to me? I felt humiliated at how easily I'd been fooled.

By the time I met up with Emma, the calls had stopped. My phone remained silent until right after we gave the waitress our lunch orders. I glanced at it, fairly certain it was Devin again, but this time the number that flashed on the screen belonged to the hotel. I thought about letting it go to voicemail, but what if it was Rob calling?

"Where are you?" Devin asked as soon as I pressed the phone to my ear. Of course it would be him instead of my manager.

"None of your business," I snapped.

"Lilli, you have to give me a chance to explain."

"Explain what? That you're a liar who spent the last few months making a fool out of me?" I blurted out, forgetting that Emma was sitting right across the table from me.

"It's not like that."

"I don't care what it's like, and I don't feel like talking about it either, so stop calling."

I hung up without giving him a chance to reply.

Emma stared at me. "Who were you just talking to, and what the hell was that about?"

"Devin," I said as I tried to come up with some sort of explanation that wouldn't make me sound like I needed to be committed to an asylum. "He lied to me about something, and I'm still pissed about it."

"That must have been some lie." Emma's gaze lingered on me as she waited for an explanation.

"After the party the other night, he kissed me." As I said those words I felt like I could still taste him, still feel the weight of his lips on mine. I shook my head to clear those thoughts from my mind. They weren't making anything easier.

Emma's eyes widened. "No way! What was it like? Is he a good kisser? He has to be; no guy can be that gorgeous and not know how to kiss; that would be a total waste."

I let her ramble on about Devin while I thought of what to tell her next. "He's a good kisser," I admitted, although, sadly, I didn't have anyone to compare him to.

"Would you get to the part about him being a liar already?"

"After he kissed me, he said he had something to tell me." I inhaled sharply before starting my own lie. "He has a girlfriend back home. It was the first time he ever mentioned her even though we've been friends for months. I'm pissed. He should've told me. It's not right to kiss someone when you've been keeping secrets and lying to them since the day you met."

"That's messed up," Emma said. "What are you going to do? You guys work together, so isn't that going to be awkward?"

I stared out the window. "I don't know. I'm sure it'll work itself out somehow." Devin said he'd stuck around Crescent City to get answers about who I was and what I was doing here. Now that he had them, there was no reason for him to stay. He had a family and friends in the Wilds that missed him and were waiting for him to return. I remembered the longing in his voice when he spoke about them. It didn't matter that the last thing I wanted was for him to go. I would tell him to anyway.

After lunch, Emma wanted to check out one of thrift stores nearby. I agreed, even though I didn't like spending any more time downtown than I had to. I was reminded why as we walked past Crescent City's crappiest dive bar on the way to the thrift store. I froze as I watched two people walk out from the bar onto the sidewalk. One of the men looked human, but the other one definitely didn't. Its eyes were black as pitch, sharp fang-like teeth matched its clawed fingers. I clasped my hand over my mouth and when I noticed Emma's eyes on me I pretended to stifle a sneeze.

"Is it okay if we do this some other time?" I asked. "I'm feeling a bit queasy right now. Too much grease at lunch, I think." I needed to be as far away from that creature as possible.

The two of us headed back toward where our cars were parked and said our goodbyes. I went home and tried to take a nap, but the creature's image lingered in my mind. Devin had explained why I could see my mother at the funeral when others could not, and he'd explained about my dreams, but I hadn't given him a chance to tell me anything about the monsters, even though I was sure he knew what they were and why I kept seeing them.

Soon after five o'clock my doorbell rang. I froze, worried about who it could be. Devin had warned me that I was in danger, yet I'd managed to make it through life unscathed so far. Perhaps he'd been going for drama, hoping that it would keep me from running off. *No.* Devin didn't seem like the type of person who would scare me just to get what he wanted, although I was now starting to question how well I really knew him.

I refused to give in to fear, so I got up to answer the door.

"We need to talk," Devin said.

My stomach lurched at the sight of him. I tried telling myself it was from anger, but I knew better. This boy who knew how to make me smile and laugh stood in front of me, holding my heart in his hands despite the fact that he'd been lying to me since the day we met.

"What are you doing here?"

His tired eyes looked stormy. "You won't speak to me on the phone, so I didn't have a choice."

I crossed my arms. "I want you to leave."

"Give me a chance to explain first. Please."

"Explain what? That while I trusted you, while I thought we were friends, you were just pretending so you could get all your stupid questions answered?"

Devin's eyes widened in surprise. "Is that really what you think?"

I turned my back on him without answering. It was impossibly hard to look at him.

"Did you know that by the time I offered to help you get a job I felt like I already knew you? The reason I spoke to you that day was because I needed you in my life. Yes, I had questions. But more than that, I wanted to hear the way your voice sounded when you spoke to me. I wanted to see what your eyes were like when you looked at me. You'd begun to consume my thoughts. I couldn't erase the image of you from my mind. You're so beautiful and strong, but at the same time fragile, too. I knew I should've found a way to walk away from you, a way to leave Crescent City and you behind, but

I couldn't. By following you, by watching you, I'd begun to have feelings I knew I had no right to have."

I wrapped my arms around myself and bowed my head, staring at my feet. "Why did you wait so long to tell me the truth?"

"Naiara left you here to keep you safe. But that wasn't the only reason—I think your mother wanted a normal life for you. I love the Wilds and I love magic, but a life there comes with burdens and danger that humans have been shielded from. You've seen it in your dreams, and you know what I'm talking about. Once I realized why Naiara left you here, I didn't think it was fair for me to tell you what I knew. I kept trying to convince myself that I needed to leave, but I never could bring myself to do it. With every day that passed, you wrapped yourself tighter and tighter around my heart. I couldn't figure out how to walk away from that. The other night, when we kissed, I fought with myself the whole night. Do I tell you everything and take the chance you'll forgive me, maybe even agree to be with me, or do I walk away and let you live the life your mother intended you to have?"

His confession made my head spin. "It would've destroyed me if you'd left," I said, my voice barely a whisper.

Devin laid his hand gently on my shoulder. "Then I'm glad I didn't."

A tear rolled down my cheek as I turned to face him. I took in a deep breath and tried to ignore the fluttering of my heart that came from my assortment of crazy emotions.

He wiped my cheek with the tip of his thumb. "Will I see you at work tomorrow?" he asked.

I shook my head. "I'm off."

"Then when?"

"I don't know," I replied. "I need a little more time to think."

Neither of us spoke for a moment.

Then Devin said, "I'll wait until you're ready." He pressed his lips to my forehead, and I wondered if he felt the same surge run through him that I did. "No matter how long it takes."

Chapter 13

AFTER DEVIN LEFT, I went into the kitchen, poured myself a bowl of cereal, and sat down at the table. Breakfast for dinner usually made me feel better, but instead of eating, I stared out the window. Dad had loved gardening. Less than a month had gone by since he passed, and the yard already looked wild and untended.

It was hard for me to imagine someone with a soul as gentle as my father's being dragged into my mother's drama. I wondered how much of her story my dad knew. Every time I spoke of my mother, my dad changed the subject without answering my questions. And now that he was gone, there was no way I'd get anything answered. My cereal turned to mush while my mind wandered, so I chucked it down the garbage disposal and headed upstairs. I picked up a book but found myself re-reading the same paragraph over and over and finally gave up.

The brief glimpse I had of my mother's face at Dad's funeral had lasted long enough for me to know that her tears had been real. If she grieved for him, that meant a part of her still cared, but if that were true, how could she walk away without a word? Did she know that she'd changed my life and my father's forever by doing that?

I rolled over on my back, groaning with frustration and opened my book again. Somehow I made it through a few chapters before my eyelids grew heavy, and I fell asleep.

A call from Katy woke me the next morning. She asked me the usual questions—how was I doing, did I need anything, and was I eating and sleeping enough? I reassured her, and when she asked me what was new, I left out the part about my mother being a witch, and still alive in a world that human beings didn't know existed. I was about to hang up when a question popped into my head.

"Katy, before my mother disappeared, did she say anything to Dad?"

"Anything like what?"

"Like that she might be in danger, or that someone might be after her?"

She paused before asking, "What brought this on?"

"Nothing. I just wondered, that's all."

"Well, if she did, Mark never told me," Katy said. She hesitated before continuing, "I wish I could tell you more, but so much time has passed, and truthfully, I think it's probably better to leave the past where it is."

"Don't worry. I promise I'm not sitting around obsessing about it or anything. I was just curious, that's all."

"All right. Well, I better go now, or I'll be late for work. Call me if you need anything."

If I was going to get any more answers about my mother, they weren't going to come from Katy, and I was certain Devin had told me as much as he knew. That left only one other person to ask—my mother. The only problem was that I had no idea how to get to her.

But Devin did, which meant I needed to convince him to take me to her.

Just before five, I got in my car and drove to his house. He wasn't home yet, so I sat on his stoop and waited. Ten minutes later he drove up to the curb, parked and rushed over to me.

"Is everything okay?" he asked.

"Are you worried that my mother's psycho husband knocked on my door this morning?"

Devin frowned. "That's not funny."

"I'm sorry. It's just that this whole thing is so crazy . . ." I felt out of sorts, but composed myself because I had questions that needed answers. I stared into Devin's eyes. "Do you swear to never lie to me again?"

He nodded and reached for my hands. "On my life."

"How do I know you're not lying now, that you're not just telling me what you know I want to hear?"

Devin cringed. "I don't know. Perhaps it's too soon to ask for your trust, but I'll find a way to earn it back, if you let me."

I could tell he was full of remorse, but that wasn't enough to reign in my anger. "You let me think I was losing my mind. Do you know how hard my dad's funeral was for me? It was bad enough that he died, then to see my mother at the cemetery. I thought she was a ghost or that I'd imagined the whole thing. But you knew she was there. I point blank asked you if you saw a woman and you said no. Did you even care that I thought I was going crazy at my own father's funeral?"

"Do you think I didn't know how much pain you were in

that day? I didn't want to make things worse by telling you about your mother on the same day you buried your father."

"That night when I told you about my dreams and those visions I get—you could've told me then."

Devin shook his head. "You were so upset and scared."

It was hard to be mad at someone who was already beating himself up. "I get it. Or at least I'm trying to."

"Tell me what to do." Devin rested his other hand on my cheek sending shivers through my body. It was only a hand, but the feeling of his skin against mine drove me wild. "Anything you ask for is yours. I'm dying inside, knowing how angry you are with me."

"I need to ask you some questions."

"Of course." He drew back and looked around, his gaze taking on a wary edge. "But not out here. Come inside?"

He unlocked his door, and I followed him indoors. We sat beside each other on the couch.

"You know what those monsters I've been seeing are, don't you?"

Devin nodded. "They're demons."

"Demons?" I gaped at him, and when he nodded, I said, "Why do I see them when no one else can?"

"The same reason you saw your mother at the funeral when no one else did. Demons exist everywhere, but here, in this world, they disguise themselves using glamour. Easier to prey on people when you don't look evil."

"Do all of them look so creepy?"

"No. Lesser demons look more . . . creepy. Greater demons take on a more human appearance, although most have more than one form. They all have those eyes, though."

I knew exactly what he was talking about. Eyes black as

coal, giant orbs of pitch so big that you could barely see the white surrounding it.

"What are they even doing here in Crescent City?"

"Demons exist everywhere, Lilli," Devin said. "They are in search of souls to feed on and will go wherever they think they can find one, whether it be here in Crescent City or the Wilds; it doesn't matter to them. And they're as dangerous as they look. You've seen what they can do in your dreams."

"They kill witches in my dreams."

"Sometimes that's what they do, and sometimes they harm us in a totally different way. It's because they want to rule the worlds, and witches are the ones standing in their way. If the Wilds ever falls into the hands of demons, this world will be next. It's ironic if you think about it. Witches hate humans, and yet we're the ones keeping them from being overrun with demons."

"That's just great," I muttered. As if seeing demons didn't freak me out enough already.

"The strange thing is that, even though you can see through demon glamour, it doesn't appear that any of them have ever recognized you as a witch. I'm certain if they did they would've approached you wanting to know what you were doing here. Witches don't venture into the human world often."

I frowned. "That's never happened."

"I'm grateful for that, not just because demons are vile, tricky creatures, but because if one of them recognized you as Naiara's daughter the way I did, you'd be in danger."

"You act like my mother is some sort of celebrity back in the Wilds," I said sarcastically.

Devin smiled. "I suppose in some ways she is. Not only

because she descends from a long line of powerful witches, but because of her beauty and the mystery that surrounds her. People still talk of her disappearance all those years ago."

"You said we look alike."

"You do, very much."

"So does that mean you think I'm beautiful, too?"

"I can't believe you don't already know," Devin replied, surprised. "It's a shame you can't read my thoughts."

He'd told me I was beautiful more than once, but that was before all this madness. When it came to us, I was no longer sure what was real and what wasn't. "Well, I can't. That's why I asked." I bit on my lower lip to distract myself. It was almost painful being so close to Devin, but, at the same time, I wanted to reach out and pull him even closer.

He grasped my hands, closed his eyes and took a deep breath before opening them again to look at me. "You're all I think about, night and day. Being around you makes me feel alive in a way I never have before. Everywhere I go, I see your face, like it's seared into my mind. I feel your touch on my skin, and your scent lingers on everything you've touched. I imagine ways to bring a smile to your face, and I dream that one day maybe you might feel a fraction of the way I do."

"Devin, I . . ." I could hardly breathe, much less figure out how to respond.

He put a finger to my lips. "You don't have to say anything."

Looking into his eyes made me feel weak. "Yes, I do," I began, and then I realized he was right. I didn't need to say anything. Instead, I inched closer, hoping he'd kiss me again. He reached for me, threading his hands through my hair as he pulled me even closer and pressed his lips on mine.

Lost in his kiss, I realized again what I'd known from the

first day I'd met Devin; he made everything better. In the few months that I'd known him, I'd lost my father, found out my dead mother was actually alive and married to a man who would kill me if he knew I existed. I'd learned that magic was real, and that I was a witch. Despite all of it, having Devin in my life made me feel like everything would be all right.

"Lilli, are you sure?" Devin whispered into my ear. "Are you sure this is how you feel?"

I looked into his eyes. "Yes. I'm sure."

He kissed me again before resting his back against one of the couch's arms. I swung my legs off the floor and curled up against him. He wrapped an arm around me. As I pressed my head to his chest I could feel it rise and fall with each breath he took and hear the beating of his heart. The rhythm of it comforted me.

"Devin," I said after a while, interrupting the perfect silence between us. "There's one more thing I need to ask you."

"What is it?"

"Ever since you told me about my mother, I can't stop thinking about her. I have so many questions."

"I knew you would. That's one of the reasons I hesitated telling you the truth."

"I'm glad you did, though." I took a deep breath and searched for the right words to make Devin understand. "Because at least I now know that I'm not crazy. You have no idea how hard it was thinking that all these years. And I've always felt like the story Katy told me about my mother just disappearing couldn't be right. Everyone believed she died. I did, too, but I somehow knew there had to be more to it. But . . . even after everything you told me, I still have more questions—questions only my mother can answer."

Devin looked at me quizzically. "What are you getting at?"

I gathered my thoughts, which was not easy to do when all I wanted was for him kiss me again. "Besides that teleporting thingy you and my mother did, is there another way to get to the Wilds?"

"There is." Devin paused. "Why are you asking?"

"Because I want you to take me to her."

He shook his head. "I was afraid you were going to say that."

"So . . . when can we go?"

"Lilli, I would do anything for you." He looked away. I clasped the sides of his face, forcing him to meet my gaze. "Anything except what you're asking for right now."

"Why not?"

"Because it's too dangerous. If something were to happen to you . . ."

I pressed on, in spite of the fear that crossed his face. "I don't care."

"Don't do this."

The look in his eyes shook me. It wasn't the first time I felt like drowning in him, but now, knowing he wanted me, too, the walls I'd built to keep him out crumbled. I reached for him, wanting and needing at the same time, feeling like I couldn't breathe if I didn't taste him again. His lips parted making room for me to deepen the kiss as he snaked his hands through my hair. Heat poured from his body into mine.

"What have you done to me?" he whispered.

I gave him a shaky smile.

Devin rested his forehead against mine and smoothed my hair as he spoke. "You've made me so completely yours."

"Really?" I leaned away from him, taking a deep breath and trying not to let the ecstasy I felt at that moment show. "Well, if that's true, then you'll do what I asked—you'll take me to my mother?"

Devin eyes fluttered closed for a second. "And if I say no again?"

"You don't understand. I have to talk to her, and one way or another I'll figure out how to make it happen."

"This isn't a good idea. You don't know what you're asking."

"You owe me." It was a low blow, but I was desperate. Before Devin could turn me down again I pleaded, "It's what I need to do."

"I suppose that means I have no other choice then." He sighed and shook his head. Despite the defeat in his voice I couldn't help but feel a little excited. "I'll take you to the Wilds on one condition."

"What condition?"

"That you promise to listen to me and do as I ask," he said. "And we leave only after you let me take you out on a proper date."

"A proper date?" I smiled at his phrasing. "Yes. I think I can agree to that."

Chapter 14

APPARENTLY, I HAD a lot to learn before our journey to the Wilds, so Devin refused to tell me exactly when we'd be leaving. On our next day off from work together, we spent the afternoon at the beach, where the plan was for me to start learning more about the world I was about to step in to.

The overcast weather meant we had the beach practically to ourselves. I spread a blanket down on the sand and sat beside Devin.

"Come here," he said, patting his lap. I lay on my back with my head on Devin's thighs and stared up at the sky while he raked his fingers through my hair. "I wish you'd change your mind about having me take you to the Wilds."

I turned onto my side and looked up at him. "Well, I haven't."

"Going to the Wilds isn't a good idea. If the wrong person sees you, we'll both be dead."

"By the wrong person, you mean Zoran?"

"Or someone who decides to tell him about you."

"I wonder what kind of bounty information on me would

earn. Must be a lot if someone was willing to sacrifice me like that."

"It's not so much money, but Zoran's favor that's hard for some to pass up. He's a powerful witch. Quite a few witches are eager for an opportunity to earn his approval. And, well, things are different in the Wilds. The rules we live by aren't the same as the ones here."

"But why would he want us both dead?"

"Me for knowing you existed and not telling him, you for being the child Naiara had with another man. And not just any man, but a human. I told you before witches regard humans as their enemy."

"Why is that?"

"You've heard about the witch trials, haven't you?"

"Yeah. What about them?"

"They really did happen. And it was our ancestors who were killed during that time."

My dreams.

"I dreamt about them," I said, recalling the fear those dreams had instilled in me as a child.

"The witch trials occurred after enough people became afraid of what magic could do, and it's the reason we live in the Wilds now and not here among humans. It's also the reason witches hate humans so much."

Things started to make more sense. "Devin." Anxious, I sat up and drew my knees to my chest. "I don't want to put you in danger."

"Don't even think about suggesting you go on your own," he said. "Besides, I have a plan." He must have noticed the doubt in my eyes. "I promise I won't let anything happen to you."

"What's this plan of yours?"

"We'll head to the Wilds after midnight . . ."

"How are we going to get there?"

"I was just about to get to that part," Devin scolded.

I didn't mean to interrupt him, but I was nervous and impatient at the same time. "We walk. At least part of the way. There are no cars in the Wilds. It's the only way to get there."

"You mean someone can walk into the Wilds, just like that? No magic needed?"

"You and I can walk into the Wilds, but no, a regular human cannot. Magic keeps them away, turning whoever gets close to our lands back around in another direction. The paths that bring people from this world into ours are hard to find. They're always in the middle of nowhere, hidden deep in mountains and forests. Less chance of being seen slipping out of this part of the world and into the Wilds that way."

"There isn't an easier way to get there?" I wasn't sure how I felt about trekking through the woods after midnight.

"You'll just have to trust that I know what I'm doing."

"Okay. Finish telling me your plan then."

"Once we get to the Wilds I'll take you to Rayden's . . ."

"Who's Rayden?"

"Haven't I mentioned him before?"

The name sounded familiar. Devin had talked about him before. "He's my closest friend, and he's family. Your family. He and Naiara are first cousins."

I'd been so focused on my mother still being alive that I hadn't thought about whether or not she had any relatives. The thought of it excited me.

"It will be the dead of night when we reach Rayden's home, but in the morning he can find your mother and make up a reason for her to visit. I don't imagine it will take very long to get your questions answered, and after you do, we'll return after dark the same way we came." His face clouded. "I worry that it will be difficult for the two of you to part ways again, but we won't have a choice. Are you sure you want to go through that?"

I hesitated, then nodded. "What happens after we come back here?" I said.

Devin smiled and reached for one of my hands. "We live happily ever after." He pulled me toward him and wrapped an arm around my shoulder, landing a soft kiss on the side of my head and inhaling my scent.

Somehow, I formed a coherent thought. "Wouldn't it be easier if you just taught me how to teleport?"

When Devin had first told me about being a witch, the thought scared me, but over the past few days I'd begun to like the idea. It bugged me that I couldn't do magic the way Devin could. I'd easily trade away my frightening dreams and ability to see through magical glamour for the ability to do something special. It was yet another question I wanted to ask my mother—why didn't I have any powers?

"Yes. It would make things a lot easier, but too much could go wrong and we don't have enough time to practice before we leave. Unless you want to postpone this trip."

"No."

Devin sighed. "I wonder who you got your stubbornness from."

"Maybe my mother?" I looked up at him with a grin.

"She's never struck me as stubborn. You're like her in other ways, though. Quiet, reserved, thoughtful."

My dad was like that, too. I'd always assumed I got those traits from him. "What else is she like?"

"What do you want to know?"

Ever since Devin had told me that the woman I saw at Dad's funeral was really my mother and not a ghost I'd wondered something. "When I saw my mother at the funeral it was only for a few seconds, but she looked so young. I think that's another reason I thought she was a ghost. She looked just like the picture I have of her, and that must have been taken over eighteen years ago. How come she hasn't changed at all?"

"Lie down and I'll tell you." I settled my head and shoulders against his chest, staring into his mesmerizing sea green eyes as he spoke. "We witches are mortals, but we live long lives, so we age more slowly."

"Exactly how long are we talking?"

"A few hundred years," he replied casually. That revelation left me speechless for a moment. "Of course, if Zoran finds out about you, neither one of us will be making it to our twentieth birthday, much less our hundredth."

I preferred not to think about Zoran. "What else can you tell me about my mother?"

"Hmm . . ." Devin ran a hand through his hair. "I've always thought of Naiara as a rather sad person. After I got to know you I finally understood why. I think her heart was broken by the separation, just like your father's was. In some ways, it's probably been even harder on Naiara because she's married to a man she doesn't really love," Devin explained. "I always assumed her pain came from her ability, but now I know there's more to it than that."

"What do you mean?" I asked. "What's her ability?"

"Your mother is a seer."

"A seer? As in she can tell the future?"

"Not in the way you think. She can't look into some crystal ball and tell you what your future holds. Her visions come when they come, and she has no control over when or what she sees. It can be quite a burden, knowing the future and not being sure if there's anything you can do to change it."

"How long has she been able to do that?"

"I don't know for sure, but most witches with unique abilities like hers don't get them until they're around the age you are now, give or take a few years. Seeing the future is too great a burden for a child to bear."

Hopefully, being a seer skipped a generation. I wanted an ability, but not that one. "Can she do anything else? Aren't witches supposed to be able to cast spells and make potions?"

Devin laughed. "Yes. Although it's not quite as simple a task as TV shows here make it seem. It takes a lot of practice and some people are just naturally better at magic than others. Like your mother. She's a Harwood witch, a descendent of the most powerful of our kind. All Harwoods have extraordinary mental abilities; they're empaths, and telepaths, and seers and they have the ability to communicate with each other using their minds."

"What do you mean by that?"

"If your mother was standing a few feet away and wanted to tell you something, something she wanted only you to hear, she could make it so you heard her voice in your head."

I wasn't sure if I thought that was creepy or kind of cool, but Devin's words brought me back to the same question. If I came from such a powerful family, why didn't I have any abilities? That question wasn't going to get answered until I saw my mother, though, so there was no point in dwelling on it. "What about you? What can you do?"

"My senses are heightened," he said. "I can hear, smell and see . . . well, let's just say I do those things very well."

"You're like some sort of human bloodhound?"

"I guess so." Devin grinned. "Although I'm not sure how I feel about being compared to a dog. Either way, I'm hoping that my ability can keep us safe while we're in the Wilds."

"You really are worried?"

"Yes and no. I'm fairly confident that I can get us both in and out undetected, but another part of me is scared that something could go wrong. I've dreamed my entire life of meeting someone like you. I never thought it would be possible and I don't want to lose you. I refuse to."

An uneasy silence fell over the two of us. I couldn't even guess what was on Devin's mind, but I knew what was on mine. I'd already had more than my share of bad luck, so things would be different now. They just had to be. Still, I couldn't help but wonder what I was getting the both of us into.

Chapter 15

TWO DAYS PASSED before Devin and I went on our date. Neither of us liked crowds, so we decided to wait until after the weekend to make plans

"I want to take you somewhere fancy," Devin said. Crescent City didn't have fancy restaurants. I tried explaining that to him. "But I want to go somewhere where the waiters wear suits and you have to get all dressed up."

I laughed. "Do they have places like that in the Wilds?"

"No. But I've seen them on TV, and I think it would be nice to go to one."

"The nicest place for dinner is the Chart Room," I told him. "But it's not fancy. We can go wearing what we have on now."

Devin agreed to the Chart Room, but was opposed to us going in our work clothes and insisted the two of us change into something nicer. We parted ways after our shift was over. He promised to meet me in an hour at my house.

I rifled through my closet for something to wear. It was too cold for a skirt, so I decided on a pair of black leggings and a long gray blouse with a diagonally cut hem. Katy once told me that my mother and I were the only two people she knew who looked beautiful in gray because it brought out the color of our eyes. When I was little, kids teased me about my eye color and say that it made me look spooky—something my dad insisted people only said because they were jealous.

I'd barely finished running a comb through my hair when the doorbell rang. I ran downstairs, smiling, knowing that it was Devin. Fifteen minutes later we were seated at a table with a waterfront view. Fancy or not, it felt romantic to be sitting across the table from him at a restaurant with the Pacific Ocean just outside our window, watching the sea lions play.

After our waitress left with our orders tucked in her apron pocket, Devin reached across the table for my hand. He stared at it, then began tracing the markings in my palm. "Do you know how badly I've wanted to do this?" he asked.

"What?" I teased. "Read my palm?"

"No. Touch you, hold your hand, sit across the table from you without having to pretend I didn't want more."

My heart did a somersault. It was hard to think straight, but slowly my mental haze receded enough for me to ask him a question I'd been thinking about all day.

"Why is it that witches can do magic when humans can't?"

"Witches have a deeper connection to nature, to every tree, every flower, the wind, the rain, the stars and the moon, to fire, and to every drop of water. That connection gives us the ability to channel magic. Humans aren't linked to the natural world the way we are. Instead, they're drawn to religion and science. Witches don't care to explain the unexplainable the way humans do. We embrace the idea that some things just are. Humans' whole lives are ruled by logic. Even love, the most mysterious and magical thing in the universe, has a scientific explanation. I still find that confounding." Devin's eyes shifted from me to our waitress, who was headed toward our table with our food. "We better talk about something else. It wouldn't be good if anyone overheard our conversation."

After our dinners were placed in front of us, and I was sure the waitress was out of hearing distance I whispered, "What would happen if someone heard us talking or caught you using magic?"

"We're not supposed to use magic in front of humans," Devin replied. "But if I ever had to and someone saw me, I would have no other choice but to bewitch them into forgetting all about it."

"What do you mean by that?"

"It's almost like hypnosis. That's the best way I can explain it."

"So if you felt like it, you could get people to do whatever you wanted them to?" I thought back to Tim's party and the time Devin had made that rude hotel guest apologize. So that was how he'd gotten those people to back off.

Devin nodded.

"You haven't used that on me, have you?"

"No, never. But even if I tried, I don't think it would have worked. Some of the more powerful witches can bewitch other creatures besides humans, but witches cannot bewitch each other. At least not without using dark magic."

"Dark magic?"

"Dark magic isn't exactly my favorite subject, Lilli. I promise to tell you all about it, but not on our date."

"Fine, but can you at least teach me how to bewitch someone?"

"It's not something that can be taught. Bewitching comes

naturally, once you're aware you can do it," Devin replied. "It is a rather convenient ability. It's helped me here a lot. Do you know how hard it is to get a driver's license or a job here? Humans have so many rules. I didn't even know how to drive when I got here, but after I realized I wasn't going to get very far without a car, I convinced Rob to teach me."

"Is that how you got the job at the hotel?" I asked. I was pretty sure they didn't have Social Security numbers in the Wilds, so Devin must've done something to get Rob to over-look that issue, or maybe he figured out a way to get one here using magic. Either way, it dawned on me how much he had pulled off in order to make a life in Crescent City.

Devin nodded, leaned in closer, and whispered. "It's also how I got you your job."

I wasn't sure what to say. I'd had a feeling that it was more than just luck that I got hired at the Tides.

"Are you mad?" he asked.

"No. It's just that . . . how did I not figure any of this out?"

Devin lips curled into a satisfied smile. "Actually, you seemed pretty suspicious of me. I had the hardest time trying to act like a normal human being around you."

"Yeah, you sorta did. But I just figured you were Amish or something like that."

"What's an Amish?"

I laughed and shook my head. "Never mind." I took a bite of my fish taco and then looked at Devin as he eyed his plate of fish and chips suspiciously.

"What's wrong?" I asked.

"I can't believe what passes for food in this world."

"Do you just want to go somewhere else?" I asked, feeling bad that he was unhappy with his dinner.

"No." Devin looked up at me. "I'm being silly, this is perfectly fine." He took a bite of a french fry and smiled.

By the time we finished dinner and the dessert Devin insisted we get, it was dark. After driving me home he parked behind my car in the driveway. The two of us got out, I headed towards the front door, expecting him to follow.

Halfway up the path toward my house, Devin stopped and tugged at my hand. I turned around to see what he wanted.

"Lie down with me," he said.

"You mean out here?" I had a jacket on, but it was still a little cold. Devin must've noticed the slight shiver that ran through me.

"I'll keep you warm, I promise."

We walked over to the patch of grass in my front yard and Devin lay down. He patted the ground next to him, held his hand out and looked up at me with a mischievous grin.

"Why are we out here instead of inside where it's nice and warm?" I asked as I lay beside him.

Devin laced his fingers through mine. "I never told you how much I love looking at the stars in the night sky?"

"No, you didn't."

The twinkling lights were like diamonds awash in a sea of coal. It was so quiet outside that I swore I could hear my heart beating. I never could control how crazily it fluttered when I was near him.

"Out here, under the stars, I feel like I'm not so far away from home."

"You miss it?" Why did that surprise me? I'd always assumed Devin was happy in Crescent City. I never stopped to think about how much he missed his family and friends, even though he talked about his best friend, his little brother Sage, and his two perfect sounding parents all the time.

"I do miss it. I never realized how different things would be here, and the Wilds really is a beautiful place. But, if you can't be there with me, it will never be my home again. You are my home now. Where you go, I go."

Awed by his declaration, I buried my face in his neck. I wanted to offer my own similar assurance, but the words got stuck in my throat. Devin was fearless when it came to telling me how he felt. I didn't have that kind of courage. My mind was racked with too many what-ifs.

"So tell me," I said trying to ignore the pang of guilt that stabbed at my heart. "What is it like in the Wilds?"

"When we go you'll feel like you've taken a step back in time. At first, you probably won't know the difference because it will be too dark to see anything. The only light will be coming from the moon and stars. But once we get to Rayden's house, you'll notice that we don't have all the technology that humans love so much. There's no Wi-Fi, no phones, computers, or TV's. Not even electricity."

I stared at Devin trying to imagine a world without those things. "Why do you suppose that is?

"I told you earlier that witches are connected to the natural world. It's where our power comes from. For whatever reason science and magic don't mix together well, and despite the convenience that comes with human technology, there's a price to pay for it," Devin said. "Besides, who needs electricity when you can use magic to light and heat your home? It's so much more fun, and there's no electricity company demanding payment at the end of the month."

"Hmmm. I suppose you have a point."

"Witches worry that embracing human technology will bring about the end of magic, and magic is what we are. It's part of our souls."

"So if the Wilds is so different, how did you learn about the way things are here?"

Devin smiled devilishly. "You're probably going to laugh when I tell you."

"I promise I won't."

"I watched *a lot* of TV."

I giggled even though I promised I wouldn't. I couldn't help it. It was still so hard for me to wrap my mind around how impossible everything Devin told me was. I sat up and turned so that I could stare down at him. It was dark out, but I could still see the smile that made Devin's eyes dance. I crawled on top of him straddling his body with my legs before leaning forward to press my body against his. I pulled him into a kiss. "Was it all your TV watching that taught you to be such a good kisser?"

He shook his head before reaching for me and pressing his lips on mine again. "No. You're the one that taught me that."

"Me?" I didn't want to confess my lack of experience.

"You bring things out in me I never realized were possible."

"Like what?"

Devin paused before answering. "Let's just put it this way. I feel like the luckiest man in the universe." He stared into my eyes. "I don't deserve you."

He was wrong. I was the one who didn't deserve him. He had a family, and he'd had a life before he met me. He would probably have left Crescent City long ago if it weren't for me. Apart from the twinge of regret I felt, I was totally and completely and blissfully happy that he was with me. "Don't say that again," I whispered into his ear.

Despite the warmth that radiated from Devin's body, a chill crept through. I shivered.

"You're cold. Let me take you inside." Even though I wasn't ready to give up our blanket of stars, I knew Devin would insist, so I got up and let him lead me to the door.

Chapter 16

DEVIN WAITED IN the living room while I showered and changed into a t-shirt and sweatpants. Just as I was about to head back downstairs, he walked into my room with two steaming cups of tea.

"To warm you up," he said, handing me a cup.

"Thanks." I took a sip, then another, as I realized he was right. The tea did chase the cold away.

Devin sat down in the armchair in the corner of my room and held out his hand. "Sit with me." I let him pull me onto his lap. "I love it when it's like this. Dark and quiet. Well, quiet for you, not so much for me."

"What do you mean?"

"I can hear the wind every time it blows, the sounds the night animals make . . . and your heart when it beats."

"Really? Exactly how well do you hear?"

"Very."

"How can you stand it?"

"At first I couldn't," he replied. "I remember when I was a kid, feeling like I could hear everything and smell everything.

My other senses didn't bother me as much, but I still felt like I would lose my mind, I was on sensory overload all the time."

"So how did you learn to get it all under control?"

"My parents knew someone who was able to help me. He taught me how to control my gift. Now I'm able to tune in to what I want and tune out anything extra. At least that's how it works most of the time."

I was too in awe to say anything, so I just sat there on Devin's lap with his arm wrapped around me. After a few moments, he spoke.

"I didn't frighten you, did I?"

"No, of course not."

"Good, because I'm about to explain something else to you. Something about our journey to your cousin's house."

"Are we still leaving tomorrow night?"

"Since I see no way of talking you out of it, then yes," Devin replied. "Remember that I told you we're leaving at night so that no one will see us?"

I nodded.

"Not every being in the Wilds sleeps at night. If we encounter one of the night creatures, you'll have to stay close and follow my directions to the letter."

"What kind of creatures?" I asked hesitantly.

"Mostly wolves and coyotes, at least that's what they'll appear to be, but more often than not they are shapeshifters in their animal forms. Like the animal they choose to become, many shapeshifters prefer being out at night."

"Are they dangerous?"

"Witches and shapeshifters do not have an easy relationship with one another. None are to be trusted or tempted. It's said that, more often than not, they are more animal than human. But they won't make an attempt to hurt you if you're with me. I'm only warning you about them so that you won't be afraid if we come across one."

"What about fairies?" I asked, after taking another sip of my tea. "Will we be running into any of them?"

Devin smiled. "I seriously doubt it. They have their own lands, and rarely venture into ours."

"But shapeshifters and witches live together?"

"Yes. It's said that shapeshifters are witches, too. Where our power comes from our connection to nature, theirs comes from a connection to the animal world."

"Then why don't you guys get along better?"

Devin touched the tip of my nose with his finger. "That's a story for another night. You need to get some sleep, or you'll be too tired tomorrow for our trip."

I didn't want to sleep because I liked talking to him. I held my instinct to groan at bay and got into bed. Devin sat beside me and stared down at me. The room was dark, but I could still see his eyes glowing.

He leaned forward and rested his head on my forehead. His hand came around the back of my head and he pressed his lips on mine. I wrapped my arms around him and pulled him down beside me, my lips never leaving his.

"Stay with me," I said.

Devin nodded and lifted his legs onto the bed. "I've seen you every day for almost the past six months, and it feels like it's never enough."

"Every day?"

"Well, I had to make sure you were safe. Somehow, I could never get to sleep at night unless I knew you were home and in bed first."

"And how did you do that?"

"I teleported into your backyard and waited for you to turn your bedroom light off, then I waited a little longer until I was sure you were asleep before coming into your room."

"And how long did you stay?" I asked, fearful that I'd done something embarrassing.

"Long enough to get a glimpse of your face, but not long enough that I wouldn't be able to peel myself away."

Devin's confession left me speechless. Had he really been that concerned for me that he would do something so risky? I wondered for a moment what I would have done if I woke up and found him in my room. The normal reaction would have been to freak out, except I don't think I would've done that. Seeing him would have probably made me happy. I rested my head on his chest with my ear pressed against his heart.

"I just confessed to breaking into your room every night. Shouldn't you be angry with me?"

"Maybe, but I'm not. I'm just curious—what made you do it?"

"The idea of something happening to you scares me."

"Besides my dad and my aunt, you're the only one who's ever truly cared about what happens to me." It was my fault. I'd never allowed anyone to get close enough to me. Not even Emma and Tim. How could I when I'd kept so many secrets locked inside?

Devin shook his head. "That's not true. Your mother cares, more than you can imagine. You'll see. But for now you need to sleep, my beautiful flower."

I didn't think I could, but eventually I closed my eyes and the thumping of my heart slowed enough that I was able to drift off.

Chapter 17

DEVIN LEFT IN the morning with a promise to return later. He wanted to scout out the trail we'd be taking later. After he left, I busied myself with cleaning and laundry. In the afternoon, I packed a change of clothing into a backpack. We wouldn't be staying in the Wilds a second longer than it took for me to meet my mother and get my questions answered, so there was no need to bring more than that.

A little after six, the doorbell rang. Devin brought dinner, and despite my nerves I managed to eat. As the sky got darker, my eyes began to dart back and forth to the clock that hung on the wall just above the TV. If Devin noticed, he didn't say a thing. It wasn't until almost midnight that he stood up from the couch, pressed the off button on the TV remote and said, "C'mon, let's just get this over with."

I ran upstairs to retrieve my backpack. When I came back down I found Devin waiting in the driveway beside his car.

"We're driving?" I asked.

"At least part of the way."

I got in, and Devin drove off. Silence hung in the air, heavy, like an oppressively hot day. I tried to think of the right words to get a conversation started, but nothing came to mind.

"Where are we headed?" I finally asked.

"You'll see," Devin replied, abruptly.

After a while he turned onto Howland Hill Road, an unpaved road that headed east toward the Jedediah Smith Redwoods State Park. Eventually, he pulled into a parking area, and the two of us got out.

Devin held my hand as we started to walk. "C'mon," he said, heading for the woods.

I slung my backpack over my shoulder and followed him. I'd hiked most of the trails near Crescent City, but it was too dark for me to recognize where we were.

We walked in silence. The only sound came from the babbling of the Smith River, which ran through the woods. We started out on a trail but then Devin veered off, pulling me along behind him. "It's this way," he whispered when I hesitated.

"Is this the way you got here when you came to Crescent City?"

"No," he said, without elaborating.

"Then how do you know we're going the right way?"

"Bloodhound, remember?"

How anyone could make heads or tails of which direction to take was beyond me, but I trusted Devin. Walking off-trail through the woods in the dark was not a pleasant experience. I could barely see a thing. More than once, I stepped wrong and cursed under my breath as I almost slipped and twisted my ankle.

"How much longer?"

"Another few minutes, I swear," Devin said.

"If this isn't the way you came to Crescent City, how do you know about this route?"

"There are pathways into the Wilds all over the human world. I found this one earlier when I came out here to map everything out."

"Will I know when we cross into the Wilds?"

"You will. There's an energy there; it almost feels like even the air is alive."

I had no idea what Devin was trying to describe until the feeling hit. Eventually, the trees and dense forest undergrowth thinned out, making the trek easier. I knew we'd crossed over into the Wilds when I felt the strangest sensation run through me, almost like a power surge. I began to notice things I hadn't before, the way the tree branches danced in the wind as if they were having a conversation with the air. I hadn't noticed any animal noises before, but now they were everywhere. Birds crowing, wolves howling; it was frightening and awesome at the same time.

"We're here," Devin whispered. "Are you okay?"

"Why wouldn't I be?"

"It may be another hour of walking before we get to Rayden's."

"I can handle it. I grew up hiking and jogging on trails, this is nothing."

We walked mostly in silence. Every so often I heard Devin whisper under his breath. I wasn't sure what he was saying and when I asked, he only reminded me that I'd promised to trust him. Despite my insistence that I could handle things, after some time I found myself getting tired. It was probably close to two in the morning, but I'd stayed up longer than that in the past. I guessed it was a combination of things that had me so fatigued. Devin took my backpack, refusing to let me argue with him that I was fine. I wanted to take a break, to rest for a few minutes. I stopped when I spotted what looked like a fallen tree. It was the perfect place to sit. Devin turned around.

"What's wrong?"

"Can we sit for a minute?"

"The faster we get to Rayden's the better," Devin said. "If you're tired, I can carry you the rest of the way."

"Umm . . . I don't think so." The idea of being carried like a helpless child mortified me.

"Just let me do this." Devin handed me my backpack and hunched over so that I could get on his back.

"No way, I'm fine," I said, and got up to prove it to him.

Devin laughed softly. "Too bad for me you're so stubborn. I would've enjoyed you being so close."

He took my backpack from me and we started walking again. I was about to ask how much farther when we reached a clearing in the woods.

"There it is, your cousin's house."

All I could make out was Devin, the stars, a hazy sliver of moon behind dense clouds, and the ground beneath my feet. Seconds later, the clouds moved on, and a beam of moonlight outlined the silhouette of a cabin. Devin led me up the stairs to the threshold.

He tapped on the door once, then paused before tapping two more times. It was so quiet outside, I could hear my own heartbeat. No longer whispering, his voice cut through the silence.

"I'm almost looking forward to Ray's reaction when he sees you."

"What if he doesn't answer?"

"Oh, he will. We have our own special knock."

It took a few more seconds, but Devin was right.

At last the door opened and a head poked out. "What in the worlds are you doing here in the dead of night?"

"Open up, I'll explain inside."

Once Rayden opened the door wide enough for us to enter, Devin pulled me inside behind him, closed the door, and locked it. From somewhere a light came on flooding the room with a soft glow. As I examined my surroundings, Rayden gasped.

"It can't be." He walked up to me and touched my cheek with his open palm before turning to look at Devin. "Is this some sort of trick, or is she who I think she is?"

Chapter 18

ONCE DEVIN FINISHED explaining everything, Rayden turned to look at me. His lips curled into a smile and he pulled me into his arms, twirling me around and lifting my feet off the floor as if we were family reunited after a long time apart rather than the strangers we actually were.

"Rayden, put her down, you're scaring her," Devin said, sounding like he was half-teasing and half-serious at the same time

"Is that right?" Rayden asked after my feet were firmly on solid ground again. "Did I frighten you?"

"Scared, no, but maybe a little bit startled."

"Things are very different where the humans live, Ray. Families aren't as close. Give her time to get acclimated."

I wasn't sure exactly what Devin meant. I made a mental note to ask him later when things had settled down a bit.

"The two of you must be hungry and thirsty," Rayden said.

I watched him as he made his way to the corner of the large room. It was obviously the main room of the house. A long table crossed the distance between a makeshift kitchen and an enormous glowing fireplace. A metal bar was suspended from one end of it to the other and a kettle hung from it. Rayden walked over to the fireplace, brought the kettle to the kitchen, and poured its contents into three cups. Devin helped him bring them over to the table.

"Sit," Rayden said, pulling out a chair for me. I was so dumbstruck by everything that I hadn't realized I'd just been standing there staring gape-mouthed the whole time.

"Thank you." I wrapped my hands around the warm cup before bringing it to my lips.

"I still can't believe this." Rayden said, staring at me. "Not once did Naiara mention she had a daughter. I understand why, but still. And I can't believe my best friend is in love with her. I'm almost afraid to go to back to sleep in case I wake up and this whole thing turns out to have just been a dream."

How he knew that Devin and I were a couple, I had no idea. And neither of us had used the L word yet. "Wait . . . it's not exactly . . ." I began to correct him, but Devin cut me off.

"It's no dream, Ray. Believe me, when I first saw Lilli I was just as shocked as you are now."

Rayden shook his head. "You shouldn't have brought her here; it's too dangerous." He looked at me and smiled to cover his abruptness. "Not that I'm not pleased to have met you. I am. But I don't want anything to happen to you."

"It was either I bring her or she would have found a way to get here on her own. She didn't give me much of a choice."

"Neither of you are to leave this house until tomorrow night when it's time to return to the human world."

"Of course," Devin said. "You should know that I'd rather die than let anything happen to Lilli."

"Well, I prefer not to lose either one of you." Rayden got up from the table. "Come on, you two. It's late; you need to get some rest. I'll show you to your rooms."

Rooms? Maybe it was custom here to sleep in separate rooms if you weren't married. I'd never thought to ask Devin about that. I glanced at Devin, he reached for my hand sensing my unease.

"We only need one room," he said.

Rayden stopped and turned around. "Is that right?"

I nodded, still shy, but also relieved. This place was strange enough. I didn't think I'd be able to get much rest without Devin's arms around me.

"Do you live here alone?" I asked Rayden as he led us down a narrow hallway just off the main room.

"Yes. I lost my parents a few years ago. My sister and I stayed on here, but she has a family of her own now."

"I'm sorry to hear that. About your parents, I mean." They would have been my great aunt and great uncle, and even though I'd never met them, I felt sad to hear that they had already passed.

Rayden turned to open the door at the far end of the hallway. A dim light to the left of the doorway that looked like a glowing orb flickered on as we entered. I laid my backpack on the floor by the entrance and turned to thank my cousin for his hospitality.

"Think nothing of it." Rayden shook his head and smiled wryly. "My best friend and my cousin, sharing a bed. I still can't believe it." He kissed my cheek, then Devin's, before wishing us a good night and closing the door behind him.

"Are we not supposed to be doing this?" I asked.

"Doing what?" Devin looked confused.

"Sleeping in the same bed together."

He smiled and walked over to me. "It's perfectly fine. Rayden was just trying to figure out exactly how close the two of us have become. You can imagine his surprise finding out that not only does he have a cousin he never knew of, but that she's with his best friend."

I was too tired to think about bathing. Instead, I slid my jeans off but left the rest of my clothes on and got into the bed that hugged the corner of the room. Devin just stood there staring at me.

"Are you coming?" I asked.

He shook his head, as if my question had pulled him out of a trance. "Yes, of course."

He walked over to the light, turned it off somehow, and lay beside me, fully clothed. I waited for him to pull me into his arms like he usually did when we slept beside each other, but instead he just lay there, rigid.

"Is something wrong?"

"No, it's just that . . . every time I've slept beside you, you were wearing pants."

I smiled and inched closer to him, throwing one of my legs over his body flirtatiously. "You don't like the way I look?"

"Um . . . that's definitely not the problem."

Suddenly, I wasn't tired anymore. I pulled him into a kiss, threading my hands through his hair and pressing my body against his.

"Lilli," he whispered when my lips left his and traveled to his neck. "I want to touch and to kiss every inch of you, but it will have to wait. A lot is at stake here. My focus needs to stay on one thing, and that is keeping you safe."

"Can you at least hold me until I fall asleep?" I didn't want to lie in bed beside Devin without feeling his arms around me. They made me feel safe, like nothing in the world could go wrong.

Devin put his arm around me, I lay my head on his chest and eventually drifted off to the quietest sleep I remembered having in a long time.

A few hours later, sunlight flooded the room through an enormous picture window that covered practically half of one of the bedroom walls. It wasn't the light that woke me, though, it was the heavenly smell of fresh baked bread that wafted into the bedroom. I sat up, looked around, and began to notice details that I couldn't when there was only a dim lamp lighting the room.

The walls and floor were all fashioned out of smooth giant wood planks. In the opposite corner of the room, there stood a giant wardrobe. The bed I lay on was covered entirely in white linen, giving one the impression that they were sleeping on clouds. I spotted an entryway into what looked like a bathroom.

I pulled back the blanket and began to crawl over to the edge of the bed so that I could peek out of the window. Devin's hands wrapped around one of my ankles, and he pulled me back toward him.

"Oh, no, you don't."

"I just want to see what it looks like outside." There was an eerie beauty to the way the light filtered through the trees. Perhaps my perception of things was altered because I knew we were in the Wilds. I couldn't help but feel enchanted by what I saw through the window.

"Things may work a little differently here, but one thing is the same—if you can see out of the window, someone can see in."

I considered Devin's warning and lay back down beside

him. "Isn't it considered rude to look through other people's bedroom windows?"

"Sure, that doesn't mean it doesn't happen, though," he replied. "And I'm not willing to take any chances."

I took a look around the room again. No clocks. "I wonder what time it is."

Devin glanced outside. "Before eight, but not by much. We should get dressed and eat before we send Rayden to look for your mother."

Knowing that I'd be coming face to face with my mother sent a wave of angst through me. I'd memorized the questions I wanted to ask her, and now I could scarcely remember a single one. I quickly washed up and changed my clothes before heading into the main room.

I noticed a seating area that I hadn't the night before. Giant overstuffed chairs that almost reminded me of bean bags, but with more structure to them, were clustered on the opposite side of the room from where the kitchen and fireplace stood. The coziness of Rayden's home reminded me of the log cabin vacation homes around Crescent City that tourists rented. Dad and I had done it once for fun. Unlike Rayden's home, those had appliances. My cousin must've baked the bread in the fireplace.

Rayden's home felt larger than it was because of the high steeple ceilings. The curtains were drawn over the windows, but so much light came through the skylights that the room was bathed in sunshine. As I stared up I could see enormous trees through the glass ceiling and I imagined for a moment that I was in the largest, most comfortable tree house ever built.

"How is this place even possible?" I thought out loud.

"Does that mean she likes it?" Rayden asked Devin.

Devin smiled. "I think so."

Rayden walked over to me, took my hand and led me towards the dining area. "Come. I want you to eat."

The table was set and covered with food. An assortment of jams in small round glass jars and cheeses sat on the table. The spread made my stomach rumble.

Rayden poured me a cup of tea while I slathered butter first, then what looked like a berry jam, on a piece of the still warm bread. I savored the combination of the creaminess from the almost melted butter and the sweetness of the jam. If all the food in the Wilds tasted as good as what Rayden had set out for breakfast I knew why Devin had been so particular about what he ate back in Crescent City.

"How did you sleep?" he asked.

"Good." I fought to think of something else to add. When my nerves got the best of me, I never could think of the right thing to say. "Thank you for letting me stay here. I know having a cousin you never knew you had show up in the middle of the night must've been kinda weird."

"Lilli, you're family." Rayden shook his head. "The truth is, I wish you could stay longer. I wish that you being here wasn't as dangerous as it is."

Devin cleared his throat. "Speaking of dangerous," he said. "The sooner we can get Naiara over here, the faster Lilli and I can be on our way."

"Don't we have to wait until night time?" I asked.

"I'm hoping Naiara might find another way for us to return home."

My heart sank. I'd hoped for a little more time to get to know Rayden. I'd always wanted a cousin. Somehow the idea of returning to Crescent City and my empty home made me sad. I wondered if Devin had known that visiting the Wilds would have that effect on me. Perhaps that was another reason he'd been so hesitant.

Rayden pushed his chair away from the table. "Got it." A second later, he vanished, and I gasped, still not used to seeing people disappear before my eyes.

"You okay?" Devin asked.

"Yeah. I guess I just expected him to use the door, that's all."

"Well, don't worry. When Rayden returns with Naiara, that's what they'll do."

"So you guys don't just pop up in other people's houses unannounced?"

"Oh no." Devin shook his head. "That's considered bad manners."

"Well, that's a relief." I took another look around the room. "So do all the houses here look like this?"

"A lot of them do, not all though. Your mother's house is a lot grander than this one."

"You've been to her house?"

"I've only seen it from the outside," Devin said. "I'm not the type of person Zoran permits inside his home."

I wondered why, but didn't ask. "It sounds like my mother has a good life here. Maybe that's why it was so easy for her to turn her back on me and Dad." As the words came out I heard the bitterness in my voice. When it came to my mother it was so hard to sort out my feelings.

"Oh no, Lilli. I don't think that was it at all."

Devin scooted his chair closer to mine and pulled me onto his lap. I leaned into him and he slung an arm over my shoulders.

"I'm scared. What if she isn't happy to see me?"

"She will be," Devin said. "It's me she won't be pleased with."

"That's just the thing. If she's upset with you for bringing me here, I'm going to feel like she wasn't interested in meeting her own daughter."

"*If* she's upset, it will only be because she knows you're safer being as far away from Zoran as possible."

I didn't want to spend my time stewing over it, so I got up. "We should clear the table."

Devin stood and carried the dirty dishes from the table to the kitchen, where he set them down on the counter. Something caught my eye: a row of pictures on the mantle over the fireplace. I walked over to them and picked up the one that I knew had to be of Rayden's parents. "What happened to them?"

Devin joined me beside the fireplace and took the photograph from my hands to get a better look. "Rayden's parents were healers. They were tending to a wounded Council member when a group of demons attacked, ambushing and murdering them. Healers are often targeted by demons. I think you can imagine why."

I was about to ask him about the Council when his body stiffened, and he turned toward the door. "They're here."

"Are you sure?"

"You still doubt my ability?"

He sounded almost disappointed as he grasped my hand and pulled me into the middle of the room.

Two quick knocks let Devin and I know that someone was about to enter. A moment later, Rayden pushed the door open and walked inside, followed by my mother. I steadied myself for her reaction as Rayden turned to close the door behind them.

I wasn't sure what I expected to happen when I came face to face with her. For the past few days I kept picturing the same scenario over and over in my head. My mother would stare at me as if she didn't know who I was at first. Devin would explain that I was her daughter. It would take a moment or two for the reality of the situation to sink in, and when it finally did, she would cry happy tears and sweep me into her arms. Of course, that was ridiculous. Not only did we look alike, but she had seen me just a few weeks ago at Dad's funeral. Clearly, I'd been overdoing it on Lifetime channel movies.

As my mother's eyes met mine she placed a hand over heart and whispered my name. I stood, rooted to the spot, speechless.

Before I was able to form words, my mother turned her gaze from me and glared icily at Devin. "You've no idea what you have done."

Chapter 19

MY MOTHER'S REACTION caused a storm of anger and rejection to billow through me. She clearly had no desire to see me, and was angry with Devin because he had brought me to her.

"Don't talk to him like that," I said. "I made him bring me here. If you want to be upset with someone, be upset with me."

"She defends you even though you've put her life at risk," my mother said, addressing Devin as if I wasn't in the room. He lowered his head, like a child being scolded by their parent.

"I'm here only because I need answers from you," I said, choking back tears. "Once you give them to me, I'll leave, and you can go back to forgetting that you ever have a daughter."

"What?" My mother looked at me like I'd just slapped her across the face. "You can't really believe that's what I want?"

"You disappeared from my life without a trace. No note, no picture, nothing to remember you by, and then you show up at my father's funeral. It was your chance to explain things to me, but instead you ran away and let me think I was losing my mind. What kind of mother does that?" I wiped the tears from my cheeks and pressed my fingers over my eyes to steady myself. I'd sworn I wouldn't cry, yet here I was, bawling like a baby.

"The kind who wants to protect the daughter she loves more than her own life."

I dropped my hands from my face and looked at my mother, studying her. How in the world did we look so much alike? People might mistake us for sisters, maybe even twins, rather than mother and daughter.

"You have to believe that if I had any other choice, I would have stayed with you and Mark forever."

"Why didn't you?" Rayden asked.

"I ran away from the Wilds because I wanted a different life than the one laid out for me. One where I wouldn't be forced to marry someone I didn't want to." My mother took a few steps closer before continuing. "I planned to live in Crescent City with you and your father forever. I prayed that, with enough time, Zoran would forget about me, that he would assume I was gone forever and move on with his life, but it didn't happen that way."

"If Zoran found you, he wouldn't have let Lilli or her father live," Rayden said.

"It was Dara who found me . . ."

"Who's Dara?" I asked.

"Zoran's mother," Rayden explained before turning his head to address my mother. "How is that even possible?"

"She has her moments of lucidity," my mother replied. "And one of those moments came after I ran away. She was determined to find me and return me to her son to make up for being such a poor mother to him. I used every cloaking spell I could come up with, but she managed to track me down anyway. I'd left Lilli at home with her father one day while I went to the store. That's where Dara confronted me." My mother's voice alternated between anger and sadness as she spoke. "She knew about Lilli and about Mark because she'd been following me around for days. I begged her not to hurt my child or the man I loved. She promised she wouldn't, but, in exchange I had to make a choice: come with her then and there and marry Zoran as I was meant to, or she would tell him where to find me."

"Not much of a choice," Rayden mumbled.

"Why couldn't you have told me any of this? After Dad died, when I saw you at the funeral, you could have come back later and explained everything."

"She never intended for you to see her in the first place." It was the first time Devin had spoken since my mother walked through the door. "Isn't that right, Naiara?"

"It's safer for her this way. I never meant for Lilli to learn about me or the Wilds or magic from you, Devin. You had no right to tell her."

"You're being unfair, Naiara," Rayden said.

"Am I?" she asked, testily.

"You may not have wanted Lilli to know the truth, and I'm sure you worked your finest magic to keep her in the dark, but it didn't work," Devin said in a controlled voice. "Not only did she see you at her father's funeral *despite* your use of glamour, but Lilli's been seeing . . . other things since she was only a child. Do you have any idea how frightening that has been for her?"

"What other things?"

"Demons," Devin said, his voice gruff.

"Wait. What? That can't be possible."

"But it is. You thought cutting her connection to magic would keep her safe, but it calls to her anyway."

"What is he talking about?" my mother asked me.

As I told her about my dreams and the monsters I had learned from Devin were actually demons, the expression on my mother's face darkened.

"You'll be more powerful than even I imagined," she whispered to no one in particular. "Devin, if you care for my daughter the way you seem to, then you must return her to her home right now. The longer you're here, the greater the risk."

I protested. "But I only just got here, and . . ."

"No buts, Lilli. I have always felt in my heart that there would be a time in the future when the two of us would reunite." My mother's voice cracked and she wiped away a tear that had begun to slide down her cheek. "I'd actually hoped it would be the three of us, you, me and your father, but I forgot how fragile human lives are. I never expected . . ." She shook her head. "The time for you and I to be together will come, but for now, the Wilds is too dangerous of a place for you to be."

"We can't leave until it gets dark. Someone might see us," I said, hopeful that I would have at least a few hours to spend with my mother and her cousin.

My mother's confused expression prompted an explanation from Devin about how we'd arrived under the cover of night. "I can't do any magic," I said, realizing that perhaps she didn't know that.

"But you can see through glamour."

"Yeah, well, that's about all I can do."

"Perhaps it was, but not anymore."

"I don't get it."

"I bound your powers after you were born. You weren't supposed to be able to do magic at all, but Devin's right, magic called to you anyway. It shouldn't have, but I believe the reason it has is because you are destined to be a powerful witch. " My mother turned to Devin. "The spell was dependent on her remaining in the human world. Now that you've brought her here, the binding spell I cast is broken. The longer she stays in the Wilds, the quicker her magic will develop. I don't know what her ability will be, but you need to be with her when she finds out. We both know what's at stake here, don't we?"

Devin nodded and bowed his head. "I assumed Lilli had her full powers already and that the reason she couldn't do more was because of her father. It never even occurred to me that you'd bound her powers."

"What's done is done. I never anticipated that one day my cousin's best friend would find my daughter where I'd left her a world away. But if you came across her, then someone else very well may do the same. Someone who wouldn't hesitate to run to Zoran with my secret. I'm trusting you to ensure Lilli's safety. She may not have been able to teleport into the Wilds, but she can teleport back out now, and that's what the two of you need to do. Now."

Rayden walked over to me and took my hand. He glanced at my mother. "At least give us a moment to say goodbye."

"While you do that, I'm going to use your room to have a private word with Devin," my mother replied.

The two of them disappeared down the hallway.

Rayden sighed. "Less than a day after I met you, and I already have to say goodbye."

"I'll miss you." I smiled, even though his words made me sad. I hadn't anticipated liking him so much. I'd grown up with hardly any family members, always wishing for more, but like so many of the things in life I'd longed for, having my cousin be a part of my life wasn't going to happen.

"You heard what Naiara said. The time will come when it will be safe for you to return."

Seer or not, I didn't have a lot of faith in my mother's prediction, but I kept that opinion to myself. "What do you suppose they're talking about?"

"No doubt she's making him swear on his life that he'll do whatever he can to protect you." Rayden held his arms open. "Will I scare you if I ask for a hug before you leave?"

This time my smile was genuine. I embraced Rayden, only dropping my arms from around him as my mother and Devin returned. She walked over to me and grasped my hands. "It's almost harder to say goodbye the second time around." She drew me into her arms. "I love you, my child."

A moment later, I felt Devin's hand on my arm. "It's time to go."

My mother let go and took the hand Rayden extended toward her. He circled his hand around her waist to keep her steady, noticing, just as I did, that she looked faint.

I turned to look at Devin.

"Before we do this," he said, "I have to warn you that teleporting from this world into another, especially since it's your first time, won't feel good."

"What do you mean?"

"It can be a dizzying experience. Keep your eyes closed."

I did as he asked.

He wrapped his arms around me and whispered into my ear, "Now."

The craziest feeling came over me. It was like I was being tossed around in a tumbler. I felt sick to my stomach, and a horrible ringing in my ears made my head feel like it was about to explode. Eventually, the sensation subsided, only to return suddenly. My legs felt like jelly and couldn't support me. If it weren't for Devin holding onto me, I would've collapsed into a heap on the floor.

Slowly, the sick feeling in my stomach and the spinning in my head started to fade. I felt Devin lift me into his arms. He laid me down on a bed.

"It's okay," he whispered into my ear. "You can open your eyes now."

"Where are we?"

"In your room."

My eyelids flicked open and, even though it seemed impossible, he was right. We were back home and in my bedroom.

"Holy crap," I said. "You were right, that did not feel good."

"It never does the first few times, and the farther you teleport the worse it is."

"I *do not* want to do that again."

Devin laughed. "You seemed pretty eager to try it a few days ago."

I sat up. "Well, I changed my mind."

"Good. The less magic both of us do, the safer it will be."

I knew Devin was right. Doing magic would only create attention neither of us needed. Still, it seemed strange to go back to the way things were after everything I learned.

Thankfully, I had Devin. He made it easier to have to give up so much.

"So what now?" I asked.

"I believe you and I are scheduled to work tomorrow."

"And you're okay with that?"

He looked confused. "Why wouldn't I be?"

"You don't find Crescent City boring?" Surely, he couldn't be satisfied with life in the mundane human world after growing up with magic and with the beauty and splendor of the Wilds. I'd seen so little of it, but the little I did filled me with a sense of awe.

"Not at all."

"Staying here with me means giving up on seeing your family."

Devin clasped the side of my face and turned my head so that I could look into his eyes. "There isn't anything I wouldn't give up to be with you."

"Devin . . ."

"I mean it, Lilli." His lips brushed mine and his hands moved to the nape of my neck. He pulled me closer sliding his tongue between my lips as we kissed. "This—you in my arms, your lips on mine, it's all I need to be happy."

I wanted to tell him that I felt the same way, but fear kept the words inside. What if he hadn't really meant what he'd just said? What if something happened to him, the way it had to my dad, and I lost him? Loving Devin scared me. It was risky, but I did love him with every cell in my body. Why couldn't I bring myself to tell him?

Chapter 20

NOW THAT THE binding spell my mother had cast on me had supposedly broken, I expected my life to be dramatically different, but in the few days since Devin and I had returned from the Wilds, nothing had changed. I waited to catch myself suddenly being able to read people's minds, or to start having visions the way my mother did. Instead, life went on as usual.

I wondered if my mother was wrong about me being powerful. If I had an ability, I had yet to discover it. I tried convincing Devin to teach me about spellcasting and potion making, hoping that might kick-start things. He only chuckled at my impatience.

"We were only in the Wilds for a short time," he said. "Now hush, before someone hears us talking."

By the time we clocked out at the end of our shift, it was dark outside. Ominous, gray clouds filled the sky as Devin and I got in my car. Ever since our return, he'd been spending nights at my house, keeping the promise he'd made to my mother to watch out for me. I didn't particularly care for being made to feel like a helpless little girl. Perhaps it would have bothered me more if didn't enjoy falling asleep in Devin's arms.

As I walked up to my front door I tried to brush off an uneasy feeling that came over me. I never did like it when the weather was gloomy. A lifetime of living in Crescent City, and I still hadn't gotten used to it.

Before I could turn my key in the lock, the front door opened on its own. Maybe I'd forgotten to lock it in the morning. It was only at Devin's insistence that I'd started doing it in the first place. Even though Crescent City was crawling with meth heads my house was secluded enough that my father had never worried about intruders. I was glad Devin didn't notice that my door was unlocked, knowing that I'd never hear the end of it.

Devin followed me inside and took a seat on the couch. "Are you hungry?" I called out as I made my way to the kitchen. I didn't register his answer because something caught my eye. The door to my dad's office was open. I hadn't been in there since he died. I couldn't face walking into his office and not seeing him sitting behind his messy desk.

If something had been stolen from my dad's office, I was going to be pissed. After walking over to his desk, I opened the drawers, not really sure what he normally kept in them, but figuring that I'd know if someone had been rummaging around looking for something valuable. After a cursory search, I was satisfied that nothing was missing.

Heading for the door, I realized that something was, in fact, gone. I turned to look at my dad's desk again. There was a faint line where dust had settled around the spot a picture frame had once stood. Aunt Katy had given my dad the frame as a present. She'd bought it at a flea market. My father said it was perfect for my graduation photo. Maybe Katy had taken it with her after the funeral, I reasoned. After all, who would break into my house and steal a photo?

I let out a startled scream as I turned and collided with Devin.

"Holy crap, you scared me."

"Sorry. What are you doing in here? I thought you were going to the kitchen."

"I was, but . . ." I stopped myself before saying anything that I knew would wind up freaking him out.

"But what?"

"Nothing. I just. I miss my dad, that's all."

Devin's lips brushed my forehead. He took my hand and led me out of Dad's office to the kitchen. I pushed thoughts of my missing picture out of my head, vowing to call Katy in the morning to ask her about it.

A few hours later, Devin and I went upstairs. We got ready for bed, and then lay beside each other in the dark. The way he brushed his fingers through my hair as I lay in his arms sent shivers through me. I thought back to the night we spent together in the Wilds when I wore nothing but a shirt and underwear. Devin had seemed so nervous then. Given the circumstances, I understood why. What I didn't get was what held him back now.

I looked up at him and reached around the nape of his neck, pulling him into a kiss before swinging my body on top of his. The warmth and strength of his body beneath mine made me feel feverish with need. His hands moved to my back, then my hips. I traced the line of his jaw with my lips first, then my tongue. Devin slid one of his hands under my shirt. It felt like silk on my skin, causing a breathy moan to escape from my lips. Just as it did, Devin snatched his hand away and twisted his body so that the two of us lay side by side.

"Lilli," he whispered.

"What's wrong?"

He stared at me for a moment and then tucked a few strands of hair behind my ear before replying, "Nothing."

It was obvious he didn't want to go beyond kissing and nuzzling. *But why?* He seemed almost afraid, like he might hurt me somehow, but that didn't make any sense. I was far too embarrassed to ask. We hadn't been together that long, so maybe stopping things from going further was Devin's way of being a gentleman.

He pulled me back into his arms. "So, you never did tell me what you thought about the Wilds."

"The little I saw was beautiful. I wish we could've stayed longer."

"One day we will."

"Tell me more about what it's like over there," I said.

"Hmmm." After a long pause, he continued, "I should tell you about the griffins."

"Griffins?"

"They're huge, powerful creatures with the head and wings of an eagle and the body of a lion." I listened with fascination as Devin described not only griffins but other mythical creatures that lived in the Wilds. Some of them sounded familiar from the dreams I'd had.

After talking well into the night I could no longer keep my eyes open and eventually fell asleep with images of winged beasts running through my head.

Some time later I woke to Devin's gentle nudging.

"What's wrong?" I asked him sleepily.

"There's someone downstairs."

"What?" I sat up, listening for the sounds an intruder would make, but the only noise I heard was the sound of my own breathing. "How do you know?"

"I can hear it." Devin's voice pitched lower. "And smell it."

"It?"

"Stay here." Devin crept out of bed without explaining.

I whispered his name, but he ignored me on his way out of the room. I prayed that he was wrong. Intruders usually carried guns with them. The thought sent me into panic mode. I tried reassuring myself of the fact that I'd lived in the same house my entire life and it had never been broken into.

A few seconds passed, and then I heard a loud thud. Devin wanted me to stay put, but I had to make sure he was okay. I got up and tiptoed down the dark hallway until I reached the staircase. Somehow I made my way down the steps without falling and breaking my neck. I felt for the light switch and flicked it on in time to catch Devin, straddling a man—no, not a man—a demon who was dressed entirely in black. As I gaped at the two of them, Devin plunged a small dagger into its chest. I screamed as the demon turned into a pile of ash. It was like one of my nightmares had come to life.

The smell of burnt paper filled the air as Devin lifted his pants leg and shoved the small gold handled dagger back into a sheath I never even knew he wore around his lower leg. He ran over to me and grabbed me by my arm. "Didn't I tell you to stay put?" he said, pulling me up the stairs.

"What the hell just happened?"

"I'll explain later." He yanked my closet door open, found a duffle bag and tossed it to me. "First, you need to pack."

"It's three o'clock in the morning," I said.

"Lilli, please," Devin pleaded. "We need to get far away from Crescent City as quickly as we can. That means we have to leave *now*."

The panic in Devin's voice was all it took to convince me. I filled my bag with clothes and a stack of pictures and important papers I kept in my desk drawer. Devin and I practically flew downstairs. He grabbed his backpack from the couch where he'd left it earlier, and the two of us ran outside toward my car.

"We're driving?"

"Yes," Devin replied in that firm voice he used when he made up his mind about something.

I unlocked the car doors remotely. "Maybe I should drive," Devin said as he saw me heading for the driver's side. "I'm a lot faster than you are."

"Speed isn't going to do us any good if we get pulled over."

He gave me a wry smile. "Bewitching us out of a ticket is the least of our problems right now."

"Yeah, well, according to my mother it won't be a problem for me either, and you don't know your way around like I do," I said.

Devin didn't argue.

There was only one major road to take if you were trying to head out of Crescent City in any type of hurry, so I headed towards the 101. We drove in silence until I made it to the highway.

"That thing in my house, it was a demon wasn't it?"

Devin only nodded.

"What did you do to it?" I asked, trying to subdue the

panic in my voice. The image of Devin straddled over that monster with a dagger in his hands was burned into my brain.

"It wasn't just any old demon, Lilli, it was a tracker demon, and I killed him."

I waited for him to elaborate. Instead he sat stone-faced, staring through the windshield as if he expected something to jump in front of the car.

"What the hell is a tracker demon?" I finally asked, pretty sure I already knew.

"It's exactly what it sounds like, Lilli. They're sent to track people down and bring them back to whoever it was that sent them in the first place."

"What was one doing in my house?"

"Zoran. He knows about you somehow. He's the one that sent it."

I gulped back the knot that grew in my throat. "You don't know that for sure."

Devin's head whipped around in my direction. "Yes, I do. There's no one else that would have a reason to send a tracker demon after you."

"But he doesn't even know I exist."

"I never should have agreed to take you to the Wilds," Devin muttered.

"Nobody saw us. You said so yourself," I said, trying to quell the dread rising inside me.

"Well, I was wrong. You don't get it, Lilli. Tracker demons don't just show up in someone's house for no reason."

"But I thought demons and witches were enemies. Why would one be helping Zoran?"

"They're only enemies until one needs something from the other. Witches and demons ally with each other when both think they'll benefit. If Zoran has turned to demons for help that means there's something bigger going on."

Before I could ask what, Devin pounded his fist against the dashboard of my car. I lifted a hand off the steering wheel and touched his arm. He turned to look at me. "I'm sorry. I know this is all my fault," I said.

"No. It's my job to protect you."

"There's something I should've told you, something I noticed when we came home from work earlier."

"What are you talking about?"

"The front door was unlocked . . ."

"Why are you only telling me this now?" Devin interrupted.

"Because I didn't think it was important. I thought I just forgot to lock the door, until I noticed that the door to my dad's office was open. But nothing was missing except my graduation picture, and I just figured Aunt Katy must have taken it before she went back to Eureka."

"So you're telling me someone broke into your house and stole a picture of you, and this is the first I'm hearing about it?" Anger simmered beneath Devin's controlled façade. I didn't know what to say. "What were you thinking?"

"I didn't want to worry you for nothing."

"Lilli, this can't happen again. You have to tell me everything, no matter how minor it may seem to you. You have no idea what we're up against."

I nodded and gripped the steering wheel tighter, frustrated with myself for not listening to the little voice in my head that warned me something was off. "I . . . I'm sorry."

A heavy silence fell. I wanted to apologize again, but instead I kept quiet to give Devin time to sort through his anger.

Driving on an empty highway in the dead of night was

eerie enough without worrying about why we were doing it in the first place. In the dark, the enormous trees that flanked both sides of the road seemed like giant ominous monsters. At daybreak, we passed a sign indicating the exit to the Avenue of Giants, a scenic highway that ran through the Humboldt Redwoods State Park. I'd always wanted to visit, but I doubted Devin was in the mood for sightseeing.

"Where exactly are we going?" I asked, stifling a yawn. "And why couldn't we just teleport there?"

"Teleporting will make it easier for Zoran to find us with a locater spell because it leaves a magical trace. Besides, I figured having a car would come in handy." Devin put his hand over mine. "Pull over at the next exit. I can tell you're getting tired. It's my turn to drive."

It was too much of a struggle to keep my eyes open, so I didn't argue. A few minutes after Devin got back on the highway, I drifted off to sleep. By the time I opened my eyes again we were passing through Cloverdale. As we put more distance between us and Crescent City I grew weary of the endless stretch of asphalt. We made a quick stop for food. I used the restroom and stretched my legs before the two of us made our way back on the road again.

"By now Zoran will be wondering why the tracker demon he sent hasn't returned with you. He'll send someone else or maybe even come after you himself. If we're lucky, it'll take some time for him to realize you're no longer in Crescent City. That's when he'll try and figure out where you went."

"And how long do you suppose that will take?"

"We're at an advantage here. You know this part of the world; Zoran doesn't."

It didn't feel like much of an advantage when I had

demons and powerful witches hunting me down, but I kept my pessimism to myself. "Do all demons go up in smoke when you kill them?"

"Yes, but only if you attack them in the right spot—right through the middle of their chest."

"Like a vampire?"

"Vampires don't exist." Devin replied, as if I was silly for even mentioning it. "Although I suppose there are quite a few similarities between them and demons. Perhaps that's where the lore comes from. They're immortals. They both prefer the dark, and a blade to the chest is usually what kills them, although greater demons are more of a challenge. Demons don't feed on blood though. They feed on souls."

"What exactly do you mean by that?"

"Demons are pure evil. They know that all creatures have a dark side, and so they tempt us to give in to it by promising to grant us our deepest desires. That's how they come to own a person, because a demon doesn't do a favor for anyone without wanting something in return. Every bit of dark magic a witch uses, every evil thing one does under a demon's influence, causes the darkness inside them to spread like a cancer until it takes complete control."

"Why would anyone have anything to do with a demon if they know what it will cost them?"

"The answer is different for humans than it is for witches. Humans aren't truly even aware of their existence, because demons use glamour to disguise themselves. It makes it easier for them to influence humans to do what they want them to. But human souls don't satisfy a demon's hunger the way a witch's does," Devin explained. "Witches, on the other hand, are fully aware of when they are in the presence of a demon.

Sometimes they even seek them out, because demons know all about dark magic and how to use it, and dark magic has always been tempting to our kind. Its power is alluring, and a person might fool himself into thinking they are stronger, that they won't let themselves be taken over, that they won't truly lose their soul, or if they do, they can simply get it back after."

Even though I was still tired, I couldn't fall asleep again. After another two hours of driving we got stuck in the most maddening traffic as we passed through San Francisco. It felt like it took forever, but eventually we were able to leave the city behind, and I took over behind the wheel again. The drive became unbearably boring, but Devin insisted that we keep going. We stopped in Bakersfield to eat and refuel. The air reeked of manure, and I marveled at how different it looked compared to Crescent City. Everything was brown, with only small patches of green scattered here and there, and an occasional palm tree. I wasn't used to seeing those.

By the time the sky started to darken, Devin was back in the driver's seat and I managed to take another short nap. I woke up as we drove past the bright lights of Los Angeles. When we reached San Diego, I insisted we stop.

"In another hour we'll be in Mexico," I said.

"Is something wrong with that?"

"It's another country, Devin." He didn't seem to be getting my point. "They speak Spanish there, and we don't."

"Fine. We'll stop here then."

I reached into my back pocket to grab my phone. With the help of Google we were able to navigate our way through the city streets until we found a hotel. Warm, pleasant summer air swirled around me as I waited for Devin to retrieve our things from the trunk of the car. We walked inside the lobby of the hotel and up to the clerk behind the check-in desk.

"How may I help you?" he asked.

"Do you have any rooms left?"

He started clicking away at his computer and a moment later he replied. "Sure, we have a few."

I handed him my credit card pretending not to notice the curious look he was giving me and Devin. After a few more clicks on his computer, he handed me two key cards.

Devin and I made our way into the elevator and up to the third floor, where our room was. He laid our bags down on the dresser and started unzipping mine, but I was too tired to change into pajamas. The two of us had been driving almost sixteen hours with only a handful of short breaks. It wasn't even ten o'clock yet, but I was exhausted. I took my shoes off and laid down on the bed without even bothering to pull the covers over myself. I could hear Devin's voice, but I was too groggy to make out what he was saying. In a matter of minutes I was out cold.

Chapter 21

WHEN I WOKE up, the covers were pulled over me and I lay in Devin's arms. I turned over, smiling, happy, but then reality hit. We weren't sharing a hotel room in San Diego because the two of us had managed to take a vacation. Less than forty-eight hours ago I'd watched a demon transform into a pile ash after Devin stabbed him through the chest.

Devin's eyes flicked open. "Tell me what you're thinking."

"Who said I was thinking anything?"

"I can always tell when something is on your mind."

"Don't tell me you have psychic powers, too?"

"I don't need them when it comes to you." Devin brushed my hair back with his hand. "You wear your feelings all over your face."

"Well . . . I guess I'm just wondering what our plan is now," I confessed.

"The plan is to get rid of Zoran. I'm not exactly sure how, but I'll figure it out."

"By 'get rid of' do you mean kill?"

"Yes. That's exactly what I mean."

I sat up and shook my head, not believing that my life had come to this. I didn't want Devin to have blood on his hands because of me, although I supposed it was too late for that. I'd always thought of Devin as gentle, but I realized that, when it came to me, he could be fierce. My mind flashed back to the times he'd lost his temper. It was always when he thought someone was mistreating me.

Devin put his hand on my shoulder, and I turned around to look at him. "It's kill or be killed. You have a beautiful heart, Lilli, so it's hard for you to understand evil, but that's what Zoran is."

"I know, but . . ."

"He sent a demon after you; that should be enough to convince you of what needs to be done."

I didn't like what Devin was saying. Not only because the idea of him going toe to toe with a powerful witch scared me, but because I knew he was right. Devin had once told me that humans and witches lived by a different code, that things were different in the Wilds than they were here, and I was finally beginning to understand.

Without replying, I crawled out of bed and grabbed my duffel bag.

"Where are you going?" Devin asked.

"I really need a shower," I said, heading to the bathroom. *And to clear my head.*

I wasn't used to staying in hotel rooms—actually I wasn't used to staying anywhere except the home I'd grown up in—so it took me a while to figure out how to get the shower running and the water to the right temperature. Once I stepped in the tub and water sprayed over my body I took a few deep breaths and relaxed as the warm water helped to smooth out some of the kinks I'd gotten from being cramped up inside the car for so many hours.

As I thought about the conversation Devin and I just had, I wondered if the predicament we were in was as simple as Devin made it out to be. What would happen after Zoran was out of the picture? Something told me it wouldn't be that easy, that it wouldn't just end there. I shuddered at the idea of spending the rest of my life dodging demons and vengeful witches. How had this become my life?

*

I'd always wanted to vacation in San Diego, but despite the sunshine, perfect blue sky and swaying palm trees, I couldn't take my mind off the reason we were here. During breakfast Devin tried to coax a smile out of me, but I couldn't muster one. He suggested a walk on the beach, and I only agreed because the alternative, staying holed up in our hotel room all day, was a worse option.

Neither of us brought the subject of Zoran up while we walked along the shore dodging kids playing in the surf. The cool water felt good on my feet and for a while I was able to let go of what had happened over the past few days.

By the time Devin and I returned to our room we were both covered in a mess of salt and sand, so I headed straight for the shower. I was still washing my hair when I heard my cell phone and recognized the ring tone as Katy's. I toweled off and wondered what I would tell her when I eventually talked to her. I could only avoid her calls for so long before she'd start to worry. A short trip was easy enough to explain, but I had no idea how long it would be before it was safe to return to Crescent City. Eventually she'd start asking questions I couldn't answer.

After I was done in the bathroom I asked Devin about trying to bewitch Katy, but he said it wasn't something you could do over the phone.

"Just tell her we decided to take a trip together," he said.

"I suppose letting her know the truth is not an option." I wasn't very good at lying, but if I told Katy the truth she'd think I was crazy, so it wasn't like there was any other choice.

"No! You can't tell her anything. She can never know what we really are." There was an unmistakable urgency in his voice.

I knew Devin's fear came from the stories he'd heard about the witch trials, but my aunt would never let anything like that happen to me. "I trust Katy. If I told her about us being witches, she would keep our secret." That is, if she even believed me.

"Humans may enjoy the idea of us, they may even like reading fairy tales to their children and watching scary vampire movies, but that's because to them we aren't real," Devin continued. "And that's how it has to stay. Like it or not, humans and magic are not meant to mix."

"Then how is it that my mother fell in love with my dad?"

"Love is always a mystery, Lilli. Even knowing what it could cost her, something about your father must have made her willing to break the rules."

And look where it got me. I was literally running for my life because of the rules my mother had broken.

Chapter 22

I SPENT MOST OF the night tossing and turning, unable to shut off my thoughts until well after midnight. By the time I got out of bed the next morning, it was almost ten. I didn't normally sleep that late. Devin was already dressed. He sat in the large armchair that stood in the corner of the room, waiting for me to wake up. He smiled as I sat up and rubbed my eyes.

"Are we going somewhere?" I asked.

Devin got up and came to sit beside me. "I thought this would be a nice place to spend the day." He handed me a brochure that read Balboa Park across the front page that must have come from the lobby.

"Do you really think it's safe for us to go?" I asked, looking through the pamphlet. "This place seems like a pretty popular tourist attraction."

"The clerk downstairs assured me that the park is quite large, and, if privacy is what we want, we should be able to find it," Devin replied. A smile spread across his face. "But if you prefer, we can stay here instead." He brushed my hair back over my shoulders. The feel of his fingers on my neck sent shivers through my body. I was almost tempted to pull him back in bed beside me.

"No. I don't want to stay inside all day." I could see that it was sunny outside. Even with the curtains drawn, the sun's rays still splashed into the room from the crack between where the curtains met. So despite Devin's offer, I got out of bed and readied myself for the day.

We stopped at a bagel shop, where we bought a few things to take with us. At the park, we wandered along a path that sliced through endless green lawns edged with towering palm trees. Balboa Park turned out to be enormous, and a bigger tourist attraction than I'd anticipated, drawing in a pretty large crowd. When Devin had said that he'd found somewhere private for us to spend the day, I wasn't expecting to have to wade through so many people to get to it. It took some doing, but eventually we found a spot away from the park's other visitors.

I lay a blanket that I'd grabbed from the trunk of my car down on the grass in a shady spot. It was a perfect day, the sun was out which made it hot, almost too hot, but underneath the shade of a tree the temperature was perfect.

"It's so beautiful here," I said. The quiet splendor of our surroundings gave me a momentary sense of peace even though I knew that there was no *real* peace for me as long as Zoran was hunting me. My head filled first with worry, then frustration, and resentment. "Have you come up with any ideas on how to get Zoran off our backs yet?"

"I've got a few ideas, but nothing definite," Devin replied.

"Isn't there some sort of magical police force that we could turn to? There has to be someone who could help us."

"There's the Council of Witches, but they don't concern

themselves with these types of situations. They're more concerned with the greater good rather than personal squabbles."

"Really? So the killing of an innocent girl boils down to nothing more than a personal problem. That can't be right."

"You have to look at things from the Council's perspective. Your mother took a huge risk coming here. Then she took an even greater risk by falling in love and having a child with a human. Humans aren't supposed to know we exist. If either of us went to the Council, they'd be more focused on making sure that we weren't exposed than saving us from Zoran. They may even view him getting rid of you as a convenient way to make sure magic isn't exposed."

"That can't be all they care about."

"No, it's not. In fact, the Council's main concern is to enforce the prohibition on the use of dark magic. Practicing it is strictly forbidden in the Wilds."

"If the Council doesn't want witches to use dark magic, then they can't be okay with Zoran sending a demon after me. Maybe if we told them . . ."

"We have no proof, Lilli. And without proof, they won't believe either of us."

"Wouldn't they at least look into whatever we told them?"

Devin sighed. "I wish it were that easy, but when it comes to Zoran the Council isn't exactly impartial."

"And why is that?"

"Remember the dream you told me about, the one you had at my house?"

"The one where that man got killed by demons in front of his family?"

"Yes. From what you described, I'm almost certain

that the man you watched die was Zoran's father. He was a Messenger . . ."

"Wait. What's a Messenger?"

"Messengers work for the Council. They do everything from taking care of their compound to protecting them. Which is why, at one point in time, almost all of the Council's Messengers were eliminated by demons. Zoran's father was one of those Messengers that got killed. After his death, Zoran's mother was so heartbroken and buried in grief that she wasn't able to care for her child properly, so members of the Council raised him as their own. They aren't allowed to marry or have children, so caring for Zoran made them very attached to him and clouded their judgment. They aren't likely to believe you, me or even Naiara if we came to them claiming their precious adopted son is in league with demons. They may even think we are trying to deflect attention away from ourselves by making Zoran look bad."

I folded my legs and leaned forward, pressing my elbows to my knees. The peaceful feeling from earlier was eclipsed by a sense of frustration at how heavily the odds were stacked against us. "Can't you cast some sort of spell like my mother did? Maybe a memory spell," I suggested, not even sure that such a thing existed. "Something that would make Zoran forget that my mother had a daughter at all."

"I'm afraid it's not that easy." Devin sat up and took my hands in his. "I don't have the same power with spells that your mother does."

"This feels hopeless." I let out a deep sigh as my shoulders slumped. "And it's so hard for me to understand. I get that my mother betrayed Zoran, but it happened so long ago. Why can't he just get over it?"

"You have to stop applying human rules to supernatural creatures, Lilli. What may seem like a long time for humans isn't for witches. Perhaps that's why we behave so differently. We cling to old traditions that humans have let go of long ago. We can be prideful, jealous, and possessive, and when it comes to matters of the heart, we follow a different set of rules."

"Which is why Zoran would've never just let my mother go to be with the man she really loved?"

"Never. Witches are tempestuous creatures, and the fact that Zoran is such a powerful witch who so many of our kind admire, worship even, makes him feel free to do as he wishes. We don't have the same control of our emotions the way humans do, especially when it comes to love. What humans here call reason, we think of as weakness, foolishness. We practically worship our mates. Zoran will always think of your mother as his. The fact that she loved another man, a human, and bore his child isn't something he can accept, even if he wanted to. People would see him as weak if he did."

I sat quietly, not knowing what to say.

"Does it scare you, the things I just explained?" Devin asked, his voice gentle.

"A little," I admitted, looking into his eyes. "You don't seem anything like what you just described, though. You're so kind and patient. I can't picture you angry or possessive."

"I've tried my very best to behave around you, but if you think I'm none of those things, then I'm afraid you'll be disappointed in me," Devin said. "There were many times when I caught a man staring at you and had to restrain myself from saying that you were mine, even though I had no right to, and at Tim's party . . ." He shook his head. "Maybe it's better

I don't tell you what I wanted to do when that boy was lusting after you."

"Girls look at you too, you know; lots of them, and I don't like it either." I left out the more colorful emotions that came over me whenever I sensed someone's interest in Devin.

"But I'm yours completely and nothing will change that. You're the only one I see, even when you're not by my side. I close my eyes and it's always your face in my mind, everywhere I go."

Devin pulled me onto his lap. First his lips, then his tongue grazed my neck and he inhaled deeply as he pushed his hands through my hair. I reached for the back of his head, redirecting it so I could press my lips to his. "My Lilli," he said between kisses.

Chapter 23

AFTER RETURNING TO our hotel room, Katy called again just as Devin locked the door behind us. I ignored my phone once more, still not sure what I would tell her. I knew I didn't have much time before I'd have to come up with a cover story. I just prayed she hadn't called work looking for me. Devin had spoken with our manager Rob on the drive to San Diego and told him that the two of us weren't coming back to work anymore, which meant if Katy called the Tides asking for me, whoever picked up the phone would tell her I'd quit. I could already picture her reaction to that.

Three days had passed since we'd left Crescent City. Devin said that was enough time for Zoran to realize his tracker wasn't coming back and that finding me wouldn't be as easy as he thought.

"When he realizes you're not in Crescent City anymore, Zoran will have something of yours brought to him so he can try and use a locator spell," Devin said as the two of us sat on the edge of our bed eating Chinese food from white take-out boxes. I didn't bother to remind Devin that Zoran already had something of mine—my graduation picture. "That means we'll need to be more careful about where we go. Since neither one of us are using magic, the spell will only be reveal our general vicinity."

"I wish I knew how to cast spells," I said bitterly. "If I did I'd use that locator spell to find Zoran and kill him myself, just to end this once and for all."

Devin's face froze. "Don't say that again. You have to promise me you won't go doing anything that can put you in danger."

"Why is it okay for you to take chances, but not me?"

"I know what I'm up against. You don't"

"Well, then maybe you should tell me."

"You're right, I should." Devin set his take-out box down on the side table. "Zoran is almost as powerful as your mother is. Besides his active power, which is formidable enough, he's also talented at spell-casting."

"What is an active power?"

"A witch's ability. As you already know, your mother's is seeing. Zoran's is telekinesis; he can move things with his mind. If he wanted to, he could throw me across this room with nothing more than a blink of his eyes."

I stared at him, dumbfounded.

"You see why I don't want you going after him on your own? If Zoran is to be taken out, we need the element of surprise on our side. Otherwise, it won't work."

"How do we stand a chance against him then?" I asked, realizing why it was taking Devin so long to come up with a plan.

"I have an idea, but it's getting late and I want to work things out in my head a bit more before I tell you. We'll talk about it tomorrow."

*

The next morning, I woke to the sound of Katy's ringtone. I reached for my phone and glanced at the number, even though I already knew who it was.

"You really should pick it up," Devin said.

Hesitantly, I followed his advice. "Hey Katy," I said, pressing the phone to my ear.

"Finally! Where on earth have you been and why don't you answer your phone anymore? I left you like a hundred messages."

Sorry, Katy," I mumbled. "It was only three, though."

"Three what?"

"Three messages."

"Very funny. My point is, you usually return my calls right away," she said. "Where are you? And why didn't you tell me you were going out of town?"

"What makes you think I'm out of town?"

"When you didn't pick up your cell I called you at home. Your friend picked up, the one you asked to housesit, and he told me you'd left town."

"My friend?" Dread crept its way through my chest. Someone had been at my house searching for me when Katy called and answered the phone hoping whoever was on the line might help him track me down somehow.

"Yes, Lilli, your friend. What's wrong with you? You sound . . . strange."

"I . . . I just woke up."

"Well, are you going to tell me where you are?"

"Devin and I decided to take a trip for a few days, get out of Crescent City. We're in . . . Portland. We drove up to

Oregon." It was better she didn't know where I really was, in case she accidentally told someone who shouldn't know.

"You and Devin?" she practically squealed. "I *knew* something was going on between the two of you. I guess that explains why you haven't been picking up your phone. When are you guys coming back?"

"Probably in a few more days." I hated lying to her. "Listen Katy, I gotta get going. I'll call you soon, I promise."

"Okay. You take care of yourself, and tell Devin I said hi. Love you."

I hung up and turned to look at Devin, knowing he'd overheard our conversation.

"That was quick thinking, not telling her where we really are," he said. His voice sounded calm, but the tension in his jaw told me he was as worried as I was.

"You were right." I tried to swallow the lump in my throat. "Someone else is already after me."

"Hey." Devin gripped my arms in his hands and stared into my eyes. "You're not alone in this."

"I don't like it. I don't like that my aunt is involved."

"It's not Katy they're after. She's a means to an end, that's all. And thanks to your quick thinking, if Katy is bewitched into revealing where you are, whoever's looking for us will head in the wrong direction."

"I only bought us time, Devin. What happens when Zoran, or whoever he sent after us, realizes we're not really in Portland?"

Devin got out of bed, walked over to his bag and pulled out a pair of jeans. "I told you last night I had a plan. It's time we start working on it."

"You haven't told me what it is yet."

"The first thing we need to do is get in contact with your mother, but that's not something I can do without returning to the Wilds. I won't risk leaving you here by yourself, so that means the only way to do it is through your magic."

"My magic? Devin, I have no idea how to use it." A small detail that had become a major source of frustration for me.

"I'll teach you," Devin said as he slid his legs into his jeans. He pulled a t-shirt out next and tugged it over his head. "C'mon. You need to get dressed."

"Where are we going?" I asked as I slid out of bed.

"Somewhere quiet where there won't be any distractions. I'll ask the clerk downstairs where we might find such a place. The faster we can contact your mother, the better." Devin started for the door. "I'll be back in a few minutes. Be dressed."

He walked out of the room before I had the chance to argue with him. I let out a deep sigh and walked over to my duffel bag. I threw on a pair of jeans and a shirt. I was barely done brushing my hair back into a ponytail when Devin returned.

He was clearly in a rush to get wherever we were going. We didn't even stop for a real breakfast; instead he drove us to a drive-through fast food restaurant. A few minutes after I finished my last bite of a greasy breakfast sandwich, we pulled into a parking lot. A wooden sign read Torrey Pines State Reserve. We got out of the car and started walking.

"It's a bit of a hike to get to where we need to go," Devin said.

I was used to hiking, and in pretty good shape, or at least I thought I was, until we got to a set of stone steps that seemed to go on forever. It was no wonder we were the only people on the trail. Eventually, we found our secluded spot and sat down.

"Have you ever taught anyone how to do magic before?" I asked.

"No. Usually, magic comes naturally to witches, and I'm sure yours will come soon, too. But, given our unique circumstances, we don't have time to wait."

"We don't even know what I'll be able to do."

"Not true. You were able to teleport, so we know you can do that. We know you can also see through glamour. Now all we have to do is get this telepathy thing with your mother going. I have a feeling that once we do, the rest of your abilities will come quickly."

"So what do I do?"

"The key is to relax, empty your mind."

Easier said than done.

Devin rested his hand on the small of my back. "Close your eyes. Block out your worries, and pretend I'm not here. Focus on the sound of the ocean, the roar of the waves as they crash along the shore."

Closing my eyes was the easy part, the rest felt impossible. I couldn't pretend Devin wasn't near me, especially not with his hand still on my back. All of a sudden I felt silly and started laughing. Devin moved his hand and I opened my eyes. He looked at me sternly.

"This isn't the time for laughter, Lilli. You need to take this more seriously."

"I am taking it seriously," I replied. "But I've never been into this whole mediation, become one with your surroundings crap."

"Are you even going to try or am I going to need to come up with another plan?"

"I wouldn't know. You haven't exactly told me what the plan is, just that it involves me getting in contact with my mother."

"I'm wondering if Zoran has confronted Naiara about keeping you hidden all these years. I suspect that he hasn't, but we need to find out first."

"And if he hasn't?"

"Then he will have no reason to be suspicious when Naiara lures him to the place I have in mind. While she has him distracted, I'll get close enough to kill him before he realizes I'm even there."

"How? With that dagger you used to kill the demon?"

"Yes." Devin smiled. "I'm very skilled with them, you know. My father taught me."

"I didn't even know you kept one of those things strapped to your leg."

"They're very effective in killing demons, as you may have noticed," Devin said. "But enough about my weapon of choice, we need to get back to my plan."

I didn't like it one bit—his plan seemed full of holes. "What if you're wrong? Maybe Zoran did confront my mother, what if he's done something to hurt her?

"No." Devin shook his head. "First of all, if something had happened to your mother, you'd feel it through your connection. And second of all, I doubt Zoran would hurt your mother, at least not directly. He won't confront her about you, either, because he's smart enough to realize that if Naiara went to the lengths she did to conceal you, you mean a lot to her. You're not just some half-human child she had as the result of a fling. Hurting you will only put her further beyond his reach, but his pride won't let him do nothing. Whatever he plans on doing, it's something that he wants to make sure your mother never finds out about."

"It sounds like you know him well."

"Not him particularly, but I know the way people like him think." Devin took my hand in his. "Come on, enough talking. Let's try again."

I did everything Devin asked me to, or at least I tried my best to, but nothing happened. Nothing at all. With my eyes closed, I blocked out everything except for the wind and the waves and the briny scent of the ocean air. I felt relaxed, my heartbeat slowed, and I emptied my mind, but that was as far as I could get.

"Why isn't this working?" I asked, kicking at the sand with my foot, frustrated by my failure.

"You have to picture your mother," Devin instructed. "You have to see her in here." His fingertips pressed against my forehead. "And you have to feel her here." He pointed to my heart.

That was the problem. I was okay with the seeing her part, but I couldn't make myself feel. Our brief reunion hadn't lasted long enough to remove all the doubts I had about her from my mind. Whether she had a good reason to or not, it didn't change the fact that she'd left my father brokenhearted and me without a mother. I'd spent an entire lifetime trying not to think about her, so forcing myself to feel a connection with her went against everything I'd taught myself to do.

"It's no use," I said, feeling hopeless. "I can't do it."

"You can," Devin insisted. "But maybe we just need to take a break and try again when you're less frustrated, and less hungry." He stood and held his hand out to me. "C'mon, let's get some lunch."

Devin tried to hide his discomfort as we headed back to the car, but I could tell when he was troubled. An uneasy quiet settled between us.

By the time we returned to our room, I still hadn't thought of anything to say to lighten the mood. I turned the TV on for no other reason except I couldn't stand the silence any more.

Devin took a seat at the desk and pulled out a map from his back pocket. I didn't need to ask him what he was doing—I already knew he was deciding where the two of us would head next. We hadn't even gotten to see the San Diego Zoo or SeaWorld, I thought bitterly, not that I would've really been able to enjoy those things, and we were hardly on vacation.

Eventually, I got tired of flipping through channels and got up to take a shower. By the time I emerged from the bathroom Devin was lying down in bed. He gestured for me to join him.

"Did you figure out where we're going next?" I asked as I lay beside him.

He frowned and shook his head. "It's hard to choose. A big city seems safer, because the more people there are the harder it will be to find us, but I'm not sure which one yet. I think it's better if I wait until the morning to decide. It's easier to think after a good night's rest."

I nestled against him and closed my eyes. From start to finish this had been a crappy day and I was just pretty much ready for it to be over.

"Lilli," Devin whispered.

I looked up at him. "Yes?"

"Kiss me."

Those two words sent a fire raging through me. One of my hands reached around the nape of his neck and I pulled him closer. The caress of his lips on mine made me forget everything. He twined his hands through my hair as he kissed me. His lips parted mine, deepening our kiss. Devin flipped me over so I was on my back. The feeling of his body pressed against mine was electric. I felt breathless as he planted kisses on my neck. My fear and worry melted away with each scorching touch.

I was so tired of being scared, so tired of trying to figure out what to do. I didn't want to think about my conversation earlier with Katy, or about my mother, or Zoran. Devin knew how to make the pain go away. His touch, his kiss, was all I needed. As his mouth moved along my neck, I reached under his shirt and softly kneaded the smooth skin on his back. He let out a low moan that I took to mean he liked the way I touched him. I lifted his shirt over his head and met his lips with mine again. He wrapped his arms around me and pressed me even tighter to him. His lips lingered over the hollow at the base of my throat, I arched my back, enjoying the way he made every cell in my body feel alive. I reached for the hem of my shirt, overcome with the need to feel his skin against my own. I ached for his warmth.

But before I could lift my shirt off, Devin tensed and began to pull away.

I reached out. "Don't stop," I whispered. I kissed him, slipping my tongue between his lips, he groaned softly. My hands stroked his sweat-slicked skin. I could feel his desire for me, but it wasn't enough to stop him from tensing and pulling away again.

"What's wrong?" I asked, afraid I'd done something he didn't like. I was new at this, and he probably wasn't, although I didn't have the nerve to actually ask him.

"Nothing. It's just that . . . we have to stop."

"Did I do something wrong?"

"Wrong?" He shook his head. "Not wrong. Terribly, terribly right."

"Then why are we stopping?" I asked, inching closer to him. "Are we supposed to be married first?"

I felt silly asking the question, but I didn't know all the rules witches in the Wilds lived by. Maybe that was one of them.

"No, that's not it. For us marriage is more about ritual and ceremony, something witches love. The bond between two people comes long before that takes place."

"Then what's the problem?" I asked, trying not to feel rejected.

Devin sat up and swung his feet onto the floor. His back was turned to me. "If we went any further, I wouldn't be able to control myself, and I don't want to make you do anything until you're ready."

"Who says I'm not ready? Maybe I am. I'm eighteen after all. Most girls my age have already had sex . . . a bunch of times." I didn't actually know whether I was ready or not—how did anyone know that for sure? What I did know was, that when I was in his arms, I felt happy and safe, and I didn't want that feeling to stop.

Devin shook his head and lowered his face into his hands. "When you touch me . . ., you have no idea what it's like. Every inch of me feels on fire. Everything about you, your touch, your scent, even the way your breath feels on my skin, it makes me feel wild. I feel like I'm not in control of myself anymore, and that scares me because no matter how badly I want you, I won't take advantage of you."

"You're not taking advantage of me," I insisted. "I don't feel that way at all."

"But I do," he replied. "Between losing your father and finding out that you're a witch, you've been through enough. You're away from the only home you've known. You're scared and confused and you don't know what to feel. And that's okay. I don't expect you to feel the same way I do."

"You don't get to tell me what I'm feeling," I said, testily.

"I wish I knew how to make you understand."

I scooted closer to him and laid my hand on his shoulder. Devin lifted his head and turned to look at me. "Just tell me."

"That bond I was telling you about; I feel it. It's like you're my forever, Lilli. You're in my blood. I'm not sure exactly when it happened, but it did. If we did anything, if we made love, and you walked away from me one day, I couldn't handle it. I can't get any closer to you than I already am until I know you feel the same."

"I know what I feel, I'm just not good at saying the words," I said, avoiding his gaze.

"Why?"

"Because I'm scared."

"Hey." Devin lifted my chin and looked into my eyes. "What are you scared of?"

"Of losing another person I care about."

"You won't lose me, ever."

I shook my head. "That's not a promise you can make. My father never planned on dying, but he did. My mother abandoned me when I was still a baby to keep me safe from some lunatic, but now he's after me, and he's not above hurting you to get to me, you said so yourself."

"I won't let anything happen to me—or to you."

"Is that even in your power?"

"You give me power I never even knew I had."

But was it enough?

At Devin's insistence, we tried to get some sleep, but that question echoed in my mind while I lay there listening to his heartbeat. Eventually I drifted off to sleep, hoping that love would give us all the power we needed to protect each other.

I woke up some time later in the night and panicked as I reached out for Devin, only to find his spot on the bed beside me empty. I sat up and turned on the bedside lamp. Relief replaced fear as I spotted him sitting in the chair in the corner of the room staring outside at the night sky dotted with lights from downtown.

"What are you doing out of bed?"

"Just thinking."

"About what?"

Devin turned his head toward me. "How to tell you what I really am."

Chapter 24

DEVIN'S LAST BIG revelation had left me stunned enough to last a lifetime. I was almost tempted to tell him to just forget it, that whatever he wanted to tell me, I didn't really need to know. Almost.

"What do you mean?" I asked, bracing myself for his reply.

"I should've never been born," Devin said, his voice flat, without emotion, as if he were telling me about the weather.

"Devin, no. Don't say that."

"It's true." He looked away, and I had to move closer to hear him. "Twenty years ago, my mother was attacked, raped, and practically left for dead. By some miracle, she managed to make her way to a healer. His name was Marik, Rayden's father and Naiara's uncle by marriage. Anyway, Marik came from a long line of healers, so his family owned an apothecary shop. When my mother showed up at his door, Marik was there with a friend. Together they helped bring my mother back from the brink of death. The friend I speak of is my father, Tibor. Except, well . . . he's not really my father."

I sucked in a quiet breath as I began to realize what Devin

was trying to tell me. He turned his head in my direction before continuing his story.

"After recovering from her injuries, my mother realized she was pregnant. It was too late for her to do anything about it, so she was forced to have me. By then, my father had fallen deeply in love with her. He didn't care that she was carrying another man's child. He wanted to help raise me, even though I was a product of rape. And half shapeshifter."

I wanted to say something comforting, but no words came. I walked over to him and put my hand on his shoulder.

"Your mother was raped by a shapeshifter?"

Devin nodded. "I don't want to hurt you in that way, Lilli. I don't ever want to take something from you that you're not ready to give."

"Devin, you're not like that man who attacked your mother. You're kind and gentle and . . ."

"Half-monster. That's what I am, Lilli, whether I want to be or not. I can't do anything about the fact that my father was a shapeshifter—an animal," Devin said, gritting his teeth.

I crouched down in front of him. "Stop, Devin. Please don't say those things about yourself."

"Even if I wanted to forget, to pretend I was something else, I can't. I'm a witch with no active powers. For a while, I think my parents hoped I would develop one so they could dispel the rumors about me, but if anything, my shapeshifter traits only grew stronger with time."

"But you do have an ability. You told me . . ."

Devin shook his head. "All shapeshifters have heightened senses. We're hunters, a characteristic we get from the animal in us. My ability is just something passed down to me by the man who raped my mother and sired me."

I heard the rage and shame in his voice. I imagined it was hard enough being the product of rape, but I remembered that Devin had told me that witches and shapeshifters were enemies. That must have made it a million times worse.

"Do you change into . . . something?" I asked. Not that it mattered, he could turn into freakin' Godzilla and it wouldn't change the way I felt about him.

"No. Although, I've never tried—and I never will."

"Do you know the man who attacked your mother, or anything about him?" I couldn't even imagine how horrible coming face to face with the man who raped your mother would be, but he was Devin's father, and I imagined there had to be some curiosity on both their ends. Although maybe he didn't even know he'd fathered a child.

"No. My mother said he was punished by his clan after they learned of what he did. He died before I was born. But when my mother gave birth, his clan claimed I belonged to them. As a child, more than one shapeshifter showed up at my home hoping to take me with them, saying that I should be raised as a shifter, not a witch. Shapeshifters aren't solitary creatures, they seek each other out, and I suppose it bothers my father's family that I want nothing to do with them," Devin said, his voice bitter.

"I'm sure a part of them understands why you feel the way you do."

"I don't care whether or not they understand," Devin said, reaching out to tuck a few stray hairs behind my ear. He held his hand in place, cupping my cheek. I looked into his eyes. "Remember the first time we kissed?" I nodded, and he continued. "I didn't even ask if it was what you wanted. I took from you without your permission."

"I dreamt about kissing you for a long time before that, but I thought you didn't see me that way," I said. "That kiss was the only thing I could think about all night."

"Earlier, when you were kissing me and touching me I wanted to tear your clothes off. I wanted to make you mine. It took everything in my power to stop myself. What does that say about me?"

"I might not know that much about guys, but I'm pretty sure you're not the only one that's ever felt that way. The important thing is, you did stop yourself, you didn't do anything that I didn't want you to do."

"And I never will, Lilli. I'd rather die than hurt you." Devin stood, and I wrapped my arms around him. After a moment, I felt the tension leave his body.

I lifted my head to look into his eyes, which seemed to glow even in the darkened room. "Are you okay?"

He nodded, dropped his arms from around me, and reached for my hand. I followed him back to bed. "You're taking this better than I thought you would. I was afraid of what you'd think of me, that you'd change your mind about us."

"Why would I do that? What happened to your mother isn't your fault. It's not her fault, either."

"Witches look down on shapeshifters. They're not supposed to have babies together. It's like I said before, I should've never been born."

"And like I said before—*don't* say that."

"After I realized that your father was human, I began to wonder if that's what made you so intriguing to me. Half-human isn't exactly the same as half-shifter, but it's the closest I've come to finding someone else like me."

"So if my father was a witch, instead of human, you

wouldn't have been interested?" I asked, trying to hide my disappointment. I was hoping there was a different reason Devin had fallen for me.

"Of course not," Devin said. "My feelings for you have nothing to do with us both being half-breeds and everything to do with the fact that both inside and out you are the strongest, most courageous woman I have ever laid my eyes on."

"Hey." I shoved him playfully. "Who are you calling a half-breed?"

Devin chuckled. After his laughter faded, we lay in each other arms silently. He traced his fingers up and down my arm.

"What are you thinking?" he asked in response to my silence.

"Rayden and my mother seemed so okay with the two of us being together. Why do you think that is?"

"Because they're different, they're more open minded than most. And Rayden and I have been friends for as long as I can remember. He's like a brother to me. It's not every witch that sees shapeshifters as inferior. Some even believe that way of thinking is wrong, but a lot of witches don't. They think witches are better than all other beings, and the more powerful the witch, the higher they're held in esteem." He paused. "If . . . I mean when we go home to the Wilds, people will talk. They'll want to know how you can let me touch you knowing what I am."

"About that . . ." The thought of going to the Wilds had begun to lose its appeal over the past few days. I wasn't sure I was ready to deal with the hazards that came with life there. "I was thinking that after this whole thing with Zoran is over, maybe we could stay here for a while longer. We don't have to go back to Crescent City. We can go somewhere more interesting."

"I was hoping to bring you home to meet my parents and my brother."

"You told me you left home because you wanted to explore the world, but that wasn't the real reason, was it? You were treated like an outsider in the Wilds. That's why you left."

"Yes, but . . ."

"Why would you want to go back to that?"

"My family doesn't treat me that way. Tibor has always treated me like I'm truly his son. I miss him, and the rest of my family, too. The only reason my parents told me the truth about how I came to be born was because they were afraid I'd find out some other way; *they* wanted to be the ones to tell me. And . . . truthfully, not everyone is unkind. It's just a few people, the ones that believe witches are better than every other creature in the world."

"I guess I never realized it was that important to you."

Devin kissed the top of my head. "You know what? It's late, we can talk about this some other time. After you, my lovely flower, get some sleep."

*

Morning came too quickly. I would've liked to sleep late, but Devin insisted that we had too much to do. We spent the day trying to free my magic from whatever spell my mother had cast on it.

Fatigued and irritable, I grew despondent after a while. "Maybe my mother was wrong," I said. "Maybe I had no magic to begin with, or maybe she cast another spell after we left her."

"No. That's not it. You need to stop thinking about all these maybes and *focus*."

But the more I tried, the more frustrated I became, and the more frustrated I became, the harder it was to clear my head. Every time I closed my eyes, my thoughts came crashing down on me. I wished I could give my mother a piece of my mind. Binding my powers had been a bad idea, and leaving me in the dark about everything had been, too. She should have found a way to warn me and let me know about Zoran.

"Maybe this just isn't meant to be," I finally said.

"Yes. It is. But you have to believe in yourself."

"Can't we try something else? How about teaching me to teleport on my own or letting me try to bewitch someone. Who knows how long we'll be on the run? Eventually we'll run out of money. Maybe it's time I try using my powers to get us some free meals." I knew I sounded bratty, which only made me even more disappointed in myself than I already was.

"Again with maybes, Lilli? I'm not hanging our lives on them. After Zoran is out of the picture, I can teach you whatever you want to learn," Devin said. "But right now, neither bewitching nor teleporting are going to get us out of the trouble we're in."

I knew he was right, but knowing that and being able to do what I needed to were two different things. Long after Devin said it was time to quit and go back to our room, I insisted that I wanted to keep trying.

Finally, I gave up and let him talk me into getting dinner and going back to the hotel.

The next morning, Devin announced that we should head for Texas. I didn't even bother asking him how he'd decided on Texas of all places. I figured it had more to do with how far away it was from San Diego than anything else. The plan was to stop in San Antonio, where I would keep trying to find a way into my mother's head. I wondered how long it would take for Devin to give up on his plan and think of something else. I didn't like that we had no Plan B, or at least not one that he shared with me.

The drive was awful. I missed the towering redwoods of Northern California. It felt like the only trees we passed were palms, and even those were few and far between. Mostly all we saw was dust and dirt. It was a long drive, longer than the one from Crescent City to San Diego. Devin and I took turns driving, stopping only to eat and fuel the car. It was almost the next morning by the time we checked into a hotel in San Antonio.

We slept most of the day. By late afternoon we dragged ourselves out of bed and headed outside in search of food. The air was thick with humidity, something I'd never experienced before. It felt like we were wading through the streets, rather than walking, and all I wanted to do was hurry and find somewhere air conditioned to escape the oppressive heat.

"What about that place?" I pointed toward a noodle shop.

Devin didn't reply. His attention was on something else. He stopped walking and turned his head slowly from side to side. He sniffed the air and then grabbed my hand.

"What's wrong?"

"Coming here was a mistake." He pulled me behind him back in the direction of the hotel. "We need to get out of here."

Chapter 25

"WHAT? WHY?"

I glanced over my shoulder to see if I could figure out what had spooked Devin. All I could see was a man pressing a woman against the wall as he groped her. They needed a room more than we did and were the ones who should've been running back towards the hotel. Then the man turned his head in my direction and I realized he was no man. He was a demon— his eyes gave him away. Something dark rolled off him like an invisible wave of evil that shook my insides. The woman he was with seemed perfectly human, though. For a moment, I was tempted to tell her to run, but Devin yanked my hand.

"What are you doing?" he whispered. "Let's go."

Back in our room, Devin made a point of double-checking that he'd locked the door behind us before stuffing clothes into our bags.

"This place is rife with demons," he said. "The air is heavy with their sick smell of ash and rotting flesh. I should've known. They're attracted to vice and I've heard that human cities are full of it."

"San Diego is a bigger city than this one, and you never complained about demons there," I protested.

Devin stopped what he was doing and just stood there as if he was contemplating what I'd just said. "Maybe it's the time of day. Still, I don't want to take any chances, we should go."

"We just got here."

"I don't care." He raked a hand through his hair.

"You're overreacting," I said. I could tell the stress of the past week was getting to him, but there was no way I was getting back in the car again. Not without dinner and not until we'd had at least a full day without driving. "There's bound to be demons anywhere else we go, too. Besides, lover boy downstairs was obviously not here looking for us."

"He might not have been here on Zoran's order, but that doesn't mean he's not a danger to us," Devin muttered.

"I don't even think he saw us." The demon had only glanced at us briefly, and he'd obviously had his hands full at the time.

I took Devin's hand. "We don't need to leave this room. We can order room service, and if by morning you sense trouble, we'll leave, no questions asked."

Devin hesitated before nodding his head in agreement. He pulled me into his arms and planted a kiss on the top of my head.

To my relief, by the next afternoon, Devin admitted he was glad he'd listened to me. We stayed in San Antonio for another two days, but spent most of it inside in our small hotel room. I was starting to get a serious case of cabin fever, and my agitation did nothing to help with the focus I so desperately needed to reach out to my mother.

Our next stop was Kansas City, which turned out to be nothing like I'd imagined. For some reason I pictured The Wizard of Oz in my mind as we drove there, but Kansas City was a big city, too, and not actually in the state of Kansas, at least not the part we went to; it was in Missouri.

We could have been anywhere, though; truthfully, the weight of life on the run was beginning to wear on us both. Every day, Devin seemed more and more on edge. I felt like I had to beg him to get into bed next to me at night. He claimed he wasn't tired, but I knew from the look on his face that the real reason he wasn't sleeping was because he was trying to figure out what we should do next. It was starting to become clear that Devin's plan to get in contact with my mother wasn't going to work.

After two uneventful days in Kansas City, it was time to get moving again. Devin wanted to remain a step ahead of Zoran, which meant he didn't want to stay in any place longer than a few days at a time, hoping that that would make it impossible to find us even with a locator spell.

I woke up early the day we were supposed to leave to find Devin already dressed.

"So where to today?" I asked.

"I thought you said you'd rather not know."

"I changed my mind." Yesterday, in a burst of frustration, I'd told Devin not to tell me where we were going next. If we were stuck in a hotel room practically the entire time, it hardly mattered if we were in Miami or Washington, DC.

"Chicago. It's a shorter drive and a big enough city that we can easily get lost in the crowd." Devin walked over to me, snaked his arms around my waist and showered me with soft kisses, first on my forehead, then my cheeks and then the tip of my nose. "We're not leaving until after we eat breakfast."

My phone rang and Devin reached behind me to grab it from the dresser.

I took the phone from him. "It's Katy. I'll call her back later. I'm not really in the mood for talking right now," I said as I pressed the silence button.

"And I'll be back as quickly as I can with some breakfast." Devin picked up his key card, and stuffed it into his back pocket before leaving.

A few minutes later, Katy called again.

It was strange for her to call back to back like that. The hairs on the back of my neck stood up. Trying to keep my hand steady, I put the phone to my ear.

"Lilli." Katy's voice trembled. "Where are you?"

I froze with fear. Something was definitely wrong.

"I told you, I'm in Portland." I made my voice as convincingly cheery and confident as I could, even though I knew it was a wasted effort.

She whispered to someone. "Lilli's in Portland, just like I told you she was."

The next voice I heard on the phone wasn't hers. "I know you're not in Portland." The man's gravelly voice was laced with poorly hidden impatience. "But you're going to tell me where you are, aren't you?"

"Who is this?" I asked, my voice quivering with fear.

The man on the other end of the phone laughed. "I'm a friend of your mother's." His tone grew more serious. "I asked you to tell me where you are, and you will tell me, *now*." In the background I heard my aunt cry out.

"What are you doing to her?"

"Tell me where you are and I'll stop."

"Please don't hurt her," I pleaded.

"I will ask one last time. Tell me where you are or your aunt's screams will only get louder."

"What do you want with me anyway?"

"I have been tasked to find you. There is someone who wants very much to meet you and see you with his own eyes."

"You mean Zoran?" I asked.

I could almost picture the smirk on his face as he said, "Smart girl. Now my patience is nearing its end. It's such a shame that your aunt has to be involved in any of this. She really is very beautiful." The lurid insinuation made my skin crawl. "Is it really worth it, getting your aunt mixed up in this when all Zoran wants is to talk to you?"

Talk? That was all Zoran wanted to do? Or at least that's what this creep he sent to look for me claimed. And even if it wasn't true, what choice did I have? I refused to let anything happen to Katy, and I was tired of hiding, tired of driving for hours on end every few days, and tired of ruining Devin's life. He'd given up so much for me, and although he never complained, I could see the toll it was taking on him. The time had come for me to end this chase.

"Fine. I'll tell you where I am, as long as you promise to leave my aunt alone." I had no real leverage, but I felt compelled to at least try to ensure that Katy would be okay. "And you need to use your magic to smooth things over with her. I don't want her remembering whatever it is you did to get her to call me. Make her think you're the cable guy or something."

"No tricks," he warned. "If you lead me in the wrong direction, I'll turn right back around to your aunt's house and start again where I left off."

"I'm in Kansas City, Missouri." I gave him the name of the hotel and the room number. He asked what street the hotel was on and I told him.

Then I heard whispers in the background. It was the man's voice and Katy's, but I couldn't make out their words. A minute later, Katy came back on the line. "Lilli!" She sounded as if she didn't expect to hear my voice on the other end of the phone. "Are you and Devin back from your trip yet?"

The fear in her was voice gone, which was all I needed to hear.

No matter what wound up happening to me, it was worth it, because Katy was going to be fine. "No Katy, not yet. I just called to say hi and see how you were doing. But I really need to get going. I'll call you in a few days, okay."

"Sure, of course, that sounds perfect."

The instant I hung up, I thought of Devin, who was probably on his way back with breakfast. When he returned, I'd be gone, and he'd be left wondering what had happened to me. He deserved to know. I rummaged through the bedside table in search of a pen and some paper.

Devin,

He had Katy. He was going to hurt her. Zoran only wants to talk. Everything will be fine and I'll find my way back to you.

Before I had a chance to finish my letter a man appeared in front of me. He stood at least a foot taller than I did and was built like a football player. His head was shaved, which added to his menacing appearance. I was so startled by his sudden arrival that I almost screamed.

"So we finally meet," he said.

Chapter 26

FEAR TIGHTENED ITS grip around my throat making it impossible to speak. The hulking man standing in front of me wasn't a demon. No black eyes. Although that wasn't the only difference. Even the demons that looked mostly normal exuded an aura that made me feel ill.

The man glanced around the room. "You're alone?"

I nodded, feeling hopeful for the first time since I'd answered Katy's call. Maybe Zoran didn't know Devin had been helping me, and, if I kept my mouth shut, I could protect him. That thought gave me some peace despite everything that was happening.

The man took a few steps closer, grabbed me by my wrist and wrapped his hand tightly around it. I offered no resistance. Even if there were a way to escape, Zoran would just send someone else.

"It's time to go," he said. "Close your eyes."

I did as he commanded, knowing what was coming next. I wasn't looking forward to it, either. Despite my attempt to convince myself that everything was going to be okay, I was still terrified. A moment later, the same sick sensation I'd felt when Devin teleported me out of the Wilds returned. I felt like my entire body was being shredded into a million pieces.

A voice echoed in my head—Devin's. "Lilli, what have you done?" it said.

My skull felt like it would explode, a feeling that quickly spread to the rest of my body. Even when it was over, I didn't have enough strength in my legs to stay upright, and I fell on the floor in a heap, panting, and dry-heaving.

"Open your eyes," a voice commanded.

I tried, but couldn't, sure that if I did I would throw up or pass out.

My eyes were closed, so I didn't see the kick coming. Someone's shoe struck me in the shins. I cried out as I grabbed my legs. The pain forced my eyelids open. As I lay there on the ground, clutching my legs, I looked up at two men towering over me.

"Why did you have to kick her, Sabin? She's on the ground already, and she's just a girl."

"You have no idea how hard this *girl* made it to find her. Besides, I doubt Zoran would mind."

So the one who'd brought me here from Kansas City was named Sabin. Not that knowing his name made much of a difference. The man next to him didn't look nearly as unpleasant. Maybe it was his slighter build, or the fact that a permanent sneer wasn't painted on his face.

Slowly, I pulled myself upright, and surveyed my surroundings. There was not much in the way of lighting so it was hard to see where I was. The only light in the room came from a few candle sconces that hung on the walls. Craggy rock surrounded me on all sides. It looked like I was in a cave, and instinctively I knew that was a bad, bad thing.

"Does Zoran know you found her?" Sabin's companion

asked. In the dimly lit cave he looked ashen. His blond hair, which was pulled back off his face and tied into a ponytail, was almost as pale as his skin.

"No." Sabin shook his head. "Do you know where he is now? I should find him and let him know his visitor has arrived."

"No need, I'm here." I turned toward the voice, but it was too dark to see much. My heart pounded as Zoran approached. As he inched closer I noticed a smile on his face, but it wasn't the kind that made him look any less frightening. He looked like a tiger about to devour his prey. His shirtless, muscled torso was covered with tattoos that appeared to be some sort of ancient symbols.

"It took you long enough to find her, Sabin," Zoran muttered. "Was she alone?"

"Yes, she was."

"Hmmm. I'll just have to find the half-breed later and deal with him then."

At the mention of Devin, my heart pounded fiercely. I should have known better than to hope Zoran wouldn't have figured out he'd been protecting me.

Zoran stopped in front of me and held his hand out to touch my face. His fingertips rested on one of my cheeks. "Naiara's daughter." His voice was cold and bitter.

I turned my face and he dropped his hand.

"What do you want from me?" I asked, trying to keep my voice steady.

"So many things," he said. "But first things first. I don't think we've been properly introduced." He turned toward the two other men in the room. "What was it again that humankind do to greet each other? Shake hands, isn't it?"

He didn't wait for them to reply before sticking his hand

out towards me. I didn't want to shake it, but I was too intimidated to refuse.

"I am Zoran."

My tongue froze in my mouth.

"Well?" he said with a slight hint of irritation in his voice. "I've introduced myself; now it's your turn."

"I'm Lilli," I said, trying to keep my voice steady. I still felt disoriented from the teleporting, and nervous. It hadn't taken long for me to realize that Sabin's assertion that Zoran only wanted to talk was dead wrong. When he'd made that claim I'd clung to a sliver of hope that it would be true, but I knew better now.

"Like the flower. I wonder who chose that name for you. Was it your mother or your father?"

"Lilies were my dad's favorite flower," I replied.

"Your *dad* . . . isn't that sweet." Zoran was so close to me I could practically feel his breath on my skin. Everything about him felt dark and dangerous. His long black hair was pulled back from his face, highlighting his broad forehead and high cheekbones. I wondered if my mother, at one time, before she'd met my dad, had loved him. He terrified me, but, at the same time, I could recognize that he was a man many women would consider handsome.

Zoran turned to face the two men in the room with us. "Sabin, Kees. I need to talk to my guest in private. Leave us now."

As if Zoran were their master, both men did as he commanded and disappeared. It was still strange for me to see a person suddenly vanish. It took me a minute to find my voice.

"Where am I?" I asked.

"We're . . . nowhere," Zoran replied with a mischievous smile.

"Why can't I know where I am? It's not like there's anyone here for me to tell."

"You're here to answer my questions, not the other way around."

As I stared into the darkness, it truly did feel like we were nowhere. I choked back the fear that crawled up my throat. "You didn't have to bring me all the way out here. I'll tell you anything you want to know. I don't have any secrets."

"But apparently your mother did. Lots of them. You see, I never knew that she had a child until just a short time ago. You can imagine my surprise."

I shrugged. "Lots of people have children, there's nothing special about that. Why do you even care?" I asked, before catching myself. I didn't want to let on that I knew about his and my mother's story.

"I care because I love your mother," Zoran replied through gritted teeth. "She is supposed to be mine, and mine alone."

"My mother's dead, so what does it matter?"

Zoran laughed. "You don't really believe that, do you?"

I did my best to appear confused and clueless. "Are you going to tell me what you're getting at, because I really have no idea?"

"What I'm getting at is that I know you are lying to me." He stared into my eyes as if he dared me to deny it.

"How did you find out about me?" I asked. It was a question that had been gnawing at me ever since Devin killed the tracker demon Zoran had sent after me.

He laughed. "That's an interesting question." He laced his fingers together and held them just under his chin as if he were praying. "Your mother has always been a rather moody woman. That's not so unusual for a seer, so I understood. And then a few weeks ago she became even more withdrawn. More than once I caught her with tears in her eyes staring at the walls with a blank look on her face. I asked her to tell me what was wrong, but your mother is a master at lies." Zoran shook his head in disapproval. "I knew she was hiding something from me, so I used a spell to find out what."

"What kind of spell?"

"*Let me see through her eyes what she hides when she lies.*"

"What's that supposed to mean?"

"I'm surprised your mother wasn't more careful. It's really a very basic spell. One that makes it so you can see what someone else is seeing, even if you're not with them. Every night after she went to bed I watched what she had been doing all day, what she'd been seeing," Zoran explained. "You can only imagine how shocked I was to see you."

I felt the blood drain from my face as Zoran explained what he had done.

"But . . . the only thing the spell enabled me to do was see. I couldn't hear a word of your conversation with her. So that is why I needed you—to give me the answers I want; to tell me the truth that your mother surely won't."

"I don't know what truth you think you know, but I'll tell you my truth. My mother died when I was a few months old, and my father raised me alone. I don't remember anything about my mother. She doesn't mean anything to me."

"We both know she's not dead. At some point you may have thought that, but remember, I watched her speak with you *and* that half-breed friend of her cousin," Zoran said, not buying the version of events I was trying to sell him. "And despite your claim that your mother means nothing to you, it's clear that she doesn't feel that way about you. She kept you a secret for all these years to protect you."

"Dead, alive, why does it matter?"

"I'll tell you why it matters." Zoran turned his back to me. "Naiara left me days before we were to be married. For a year I lived in torment, worried that she was out there somewhere, hurt or afraid, maybe even dead. I scoured the Wilds searching for her, I even entered the fairy lands, but there was no trace of her anywhere. I was sure I'd lost her for good. And then she returned to me with no explanation. Our reunion wasn't the joyous occasion it should have been, though. Naira came back to me a different person. She was quiet, withdrawn, her passion for me nothing like it had been. All these years I assumed she'd been through some sort of trauma she didn't want to relive by telling me. I treated her like glass, always careful not to break her. And then I found out about you and realized what a fool I've been."

He didn't seem to know about his very own mother forcing mine to return to him.

"You should just let this go. My father is dead, and my mother is married to you. Why can't you forget you ever found out about me and let us both go back to our lives?"

Zoran glared at me, his face a mask of anger. "Are you always this simple?"

"I don't know what you want from me. It's not like I asked to be a part of this stupid love triangle of yours. I'm not the one who betrayed you and broke your heart."

"You're right. You may not have asked to be a part of this, but still, you are," he said. "You know the funny thing is, if your father hadn't died, I probably would've never uncovered her secrets. It was her mourning for him that roused my suspicion and caused me to cast the spell that led me to you."

Zoran took a step towards me and studied my face. When he spoke again, his voice sounded sad. "You look so much like your mother. It makes it almost hard to hate you. Almost."

"You have no reason to hate me. I haven't done anything to you."

"You were born," Zoran said, his words laced with anger. "Your mother was supposed to be *mine*. The child she gave birth to was supposed to be ours. In all these years we've been together, she never bore me a child, because she already had one with another man. You are all she wanted."

"You hate me just for being born? That doesn't make any sense."

"Picture your half-breed with another woman. Your enemy, no less. Picture him kissing her, touching her, loving her. See his woman with a baby in her arms, their baby. How does that make you feel?"

I gritted my teeth. Just the thought of it made me feel like someone was tearing my heart into tiny little pieces.

Zoran saw my response and laughed. "Not so hard to understand my anger after all, is it?"

"I would be angry, but I wouldn't . . ."

"The woman I have loved, for as long as I can remember, bore another man's child. And not just any man, she chose our enemy, a human whose ancestors were responsible for torturing and murdering our kind," Zoran said, cutting me off. His voice boomed, and within the walls of the cave, an eerie echo made his tone even more intimidating. "She didn't just deceive me, she broke the Council's rules and betrayed our whole kind. I bet she never told your father what she really is. He wouldn't have laid a finger on her if knew. Humankind hate witches almost as much as we hate them."

"Don't speak about my father as if you knew him, because you didn't."

"Naiara has spent a very long time protecting you and your father instead of telling me the truth. It appears that she loved the two of you more than she ever loved me." There was a bitter edge to his voice. "I cannot simply forget that not only did she choose someone else over me, but she also had his child."

"I'm sorry for what she did to you," I said, sincerely. I could see that he was brokenhearted, and a part of me understood. "You say she chose my father and me over you, but that's not true. She left us behind. I grew up without a mother, and my dad never got over her."

"She left you to save you. If I would have found her, and one way or another I would have, I would have broken your father and left him in pieces on the side of the road for the crows to eat. And surely you understand, but I could not have helped your mother raise another man's child."

"So what now?" My sympathy toward him evaporated. Devin was right, I needed to stop looking at things the way I used to. The rules here were different. Devin had tried explaining things to me as best he could, but being told something and seeing it with your own eyes were two different things.

"What now? You should not even exist!" Zoran shouted. "Your father took advantage of Naiara, seducing her and forcing her to have an unnatural child. You are an abomination."

"No, she loved my father," I said, without even trying to hide my outrage. "He *did not* take advantage of her."

"And you know this how?"

"Because my father was a kind and gentle person, not a monster, like you. If my mother ran away from you, it's because you chased her off."

"If I'm a monster, it's because Naiara turned me into one." Zoran gripped my chin in his hand. I tried to shake myself loose, but he was too strong. "You must get your fire from the human. Naiara is a lot more timid than you. It's one of the things I've always loved about her."

"I wouldn't know," I said, folding my arms across my chest and taking a step back. "You got your answers. Now let me go."

"We're not finished yet."

"What else do you want from me?"

"Is all humankind in such a rush?" Zoran taunted. "You will know what I intend when I am ready. For now, sit, relax, I'm sorry this place isn't more inviting, but Kees will return with some food for you. I wouldn't want to be accused of being a less than gracious host."

He was gone as soon as the words left his mouth, and I found myself alone. I stumbled backwards, using the wall behind me to brace myself. There had to be a way out. But even if I found it, what then? I had no idea how to navigate my way around wherever it was Sabin had brought me. I knew my cell phone would be useless. But sitting around waiting for Zoran to come back seemed like the worst of all plans.

Slowly, I put one foot in front of the other and started walking, hoping that eventually I'd find a way to escape. The farther I headed away from where I'd started, the more the light dimmed. Eventually, I stepped into complete darkness and had to walk with my arms in front of me to make sure I didn't bump into anything.

Exhaustion chipped away at my resolve. It seemed like no matter which direction I headed in, I always wound up back in the same dimly lit room I had been brought to by Sabin. It occurred to me that perhaps the only way out was the same way I'd gotten in. Problem was I'd never tried to teleport on my own.

But what was the worst that could happen?

I closed my eyes and pictured myself in Devin's arms, hoping that that's where I'd wind up. Nothing happened at all. I tried picturing something else—my bedroom—but I'd barely begun to focus on it when I heard soft laughter.

"That's not going to work, you know."

I opened my eyes to find Kees standing in front of me with his arms folded across his chest.

"What do you mean?"

"You may only be half-witch, but do you really think Zoran would have left you without making certain you couldn't teleport out of here?"

"How did he do that?"

"With a blocking spell."

"Just great," I muttered under my breath. "What do you want? If you came back to gloat, then you can just leave."

"Don't be so rude," he replied. "I brought you something to eat."

"I don't want it."

"Suit yourself." He sat down in front of me on the ground, crossed his legs and put the plate he'd brought with him on his lap. As he began to eat, the smell of spiced meat made my stomach grumble. I glanced at the food, meat and potatoes glistening with gravy, and realized that the reason my stomach was making so much noise was because I hadn't eaten since the day before.

I stared at Kees while he enjoyed the meal that was meant for me.

"Do you get off on keeping girls prisoner?"

He shrugged his shoulders and kept eating.

"What does Zoran want from me? Your friend Sabin said he just wanted to talk, but that's not true, is it?

"Whatever plans Zoran has for you, he hasn't shared them with me," Kees said between mouthfuls of food.

"Don't you see how wrong this is, keeping me here against my will?"

Kees put the plate on the floor and wiped his hands on his pants before replying. "In life we are asked to make many choices. They aren't always easy, but they must be made anyway."

"What's that supposed to mean?" I rolled my eyes, annoyed at his non-answer.

"Zoran is a powerful man. If I have to choose between being his friend or his enemy, then I choose friend. He is one witch I don't want to be on the wrong side of."

"So that's it. You do whatever he asks so he won't be angry with you? You know what that makes you, don't you?"

"Tell me. What does it make me?"

"It makes you a coward."

He shrugged. "A very *alive* coward, which is more than I can say for others who have crossed him."

I dropped my head down, feeling despondent and hopeless. There was no point in trying to reason with Kees. He'd made his choice, and it wasn't going to be helping me.

I turned my back to him. He reached out to touch my leg and I looked over my shoulder to see what he wanted. "For what it's worth, I wish Zoran would just forget he ever learned of you. He's completely lost his mind ever since he found out your mother gave birth to another man's child. I mean he wasn't exactly nice before, but he's downright mad now."

"Then help me get out of here," I said, hoping I could find a way to reach him. "You can tell Zoran that I figured out how to teleport out of here and escaped on my own."

"No." He shook his head. "It won't work. Zoran will know I helped you by breaking his blocking spell, and he would kill me for it. When he's determined, nothing stands in his way."

"There's no way out of this for me, is there?" I said, more to myself than Kees. I was close to tears, and before I could stop myself from crying, a tear rolled down my cheek.

Kees didn't reply, but his expression softened. "Don't you have someone who cares about you? Someone who would be devastated if they lost you?" I asked.

Kees looked pensive. "I suppose I do."

"My Aunt Katy—she's my father's sister—and he died not that long ago. I'm the only family she has left, it would kill her if she lost me, too," I said figuring I would garner more sympathy if I didn't mention Devin's name, since he was on Zoran's hit list.

"There's nothing I can do to help you. Zoran would kill me, and no offense, but I'm not sacrificing myself for you."

"At least tell me where I am," I pleaded. The knowledge wouldn't make any difference, but I hated not knowing and the sense of helplessness that came with it.

Kees leaned in and spoke softly, as if he were afraid of being overheard, "Zoran doesn't want you to know. He's afraid your mother will find a way to communicate with you, and that you'll tell her that you're being kept in the Void."

"The what?"

He held a finger to his lips. "Shhh."

I looked around to be sure we were alone. Being in a dark cave was enough to make anyone jumpy, I supposed.

"What is he going to do to me?" I asked.

"I already told you that he hasn't shared his plans with me."

"Would you tell me if he had?"

He shook his head. "What good would it do to know anyway?"

"Is he going to kill me?" I asked, trying to keep my voice even. I didn't want to give Kees the satisfaction of knowing how scared I was.

"No, I don't think so."

"And what makes you say that?"

"Because I'm pretty sure if Zoran wanted to kill you, you would already be dead."

*

Chapter 27

NERVOUS ENERGY COURSED through me. I got up and started pacing, not that it helped much.

"You're making me dizzy," Kees barked after a while. "Would you just sit back down already?"

"If you don't like it, then leave," I snapped.

"Zoran asked me to wait with you until he returned, so I won't be going anywhere."

"And when exactly is that supposed to happen?" I couldn't be sure, but it seemed like at least a few hours had passed since Zoran had left me alone in the cave. I wasn't eager to see him again, but sitting around in a dark cave wondering what was going to happen made me feel crazy.

"He didn't tell me."

I sighed and sat on the cold, dirty ground. I didn't really care that I was making Kees dizzy, but I was getting tired.

The two of us sat in silence for a while until I couldn't stand it anymore. "So you and Sabin are witches?" I asked, hoping that conversation would take my mind off my fears.

"Of course we are."

"Can you do anything cool?"

Kees looked confused. "Cool?"

"You know . . . something amazing."

He stood and gave me a quick bow. "Kees Ladd, expert illusionist." As soon as the words left his lips, the cave transformed into a tropical paradise, complete with sandy beach and palm trees.

"Holy crap," I said, turning to take in my new surroundings.

"None of it's real," Kees said after a while, and once more the two of us were plunged into darkness.

"Can you do it again? I'd much rather wait for Zoran on a beach than in a cave."

"I don't think he'd be very happy if I made things more comfortable for you."

"You're no fun," I grumbled.

Kees took a few steps closer to me. I looked at him quizzically, wondering what he wanted.

"You really do look like your mother," he said.

"So you know her?"

He nodded. "Who doesn't? Naiara sort of stands out, even in a crowd. She's beautiful, like you, but Naiara is more than that. She's also very kind." Kees shook his head. "If she knew what I was doing . . ."

Before Kees had a chance to finish, Zoran reappeared with Sabin at his side—I'd felt their presence as they arrived and turned to see the two of them walking toward me.

"It's time," Zoran announced.

"Time for what?" I asked.

He ignored me. I turned to Kees to see if he'd clue me in, but he just shrugged his shoulders.

While Sabin stood beside Kees, Zoran walked over to one of the cave walls and began a series of hand gestures that looked like he was painting. When he was done, he walked past me and across to another part of the wall. He did this five times without saying a word.

Kees and Sabin stood quietly, but after Zoran finished his painting, the expression on Kees's face changed.

Zoran strode back to the middle of the cave. "Come, Kees, Sabin, join me." He held out his hands. Sabin readily took one, but Kees, who now wore a horrified expression on his face, didn't move.

"No, Zoran. You can't do this," Kees said, his voice barely audible.

Zoran's face contorted in anger. "What did you say?"

"I . . . I think this is a bad idea," he stammered.

"Did I ask for your opinion?"

"If the Council finds out I was a part of this . . ."

"I already told you, you don't need to worry about the Council. I'll deal with them."

"You never said anything about summoning . . ."

Before Kees had a chance to finish what he was trying to say, Zoran moved his head ever so slightly, and Kees's body went flying through the air until he collided with one of the cave's walls. He fell to the ground with a loud thud.

"What did you do to him?!" I shrieked as I ran towards Kees's body. He lay in a heap on the floor, unmoving. I worried that he was dead or had serious injuries. I only managed to take a few steps before I also felt myself flying through the air. It was the strangest feeling—having no control over my body. I tried to scream but couldn't make a sound, and landed on the ground, clutching at my aching body. *Zoran's power.* I remembered when Devin had told me what Zoran could do, he was a powerful telekinetic. Powerful enough to send both Kees and I flying through the air.

"Have the two of you become friends?" Zoran said, sarcastically.

Kees managed to prop himself up and was trying to get back on his feet. He dusted himself off and turned to Zoran.

"Were you saying something?" Zoran asked him.

"No." Kees shook his head. "Nothing."

"Good. That means we're ready to get started then?" Zoran held his hand out, and despite the reluctant expression on Kees's face, he took it.

Somehow, I managed to get back on my feet. Now that I had personally experienced Zoran's ability, I wondered what chance I had to save myself. I felt doomed. Whatever plans Zoran had for me seemed to be moving full speed ahead, and it didn't seem like there was anything anyone could do to save me. Sabin seemed to worship Zoran, Kees clearly feared him, and my mother and Devin—who knew where they were?

I stood and watched, not knowing what else to do. A sharp pain stabbed at my head. I pressed my fingers against my temples. Thankfully, the pain subsided after a few seconds. Zoran began to chant words I didn't recognize. Sabin and Kees repeated after him. Nothing happened at first, but then a faint glow appeared on the ground. The more they chanted, the brighter the lines on the floor glowed, until I finally realized what Zoran had been doing when he was making his wall drawings. The glow in the cave took on a distinct shape, resolving itself into a stylized pentagram that curled across the walls and floor. A shiver ran through me as I remembered that a pentagram was a demonic symbol. Why was Zoran summoning demons?

The pentagram continued to glow and suddenly a flame arose in the middle of it, followed by a swirl of dark smoke from which a man emerged. I wasn't sure what I'd expected, but the man who stood in the middle of the pentagram looked nothing like the demons I'd been seeing since I was a child. His dark hair was smoothed back off his forehead. He ran a hand through it before straightening his jacket. He was impeccably dressed, and if it weren't for his black eyes, he could easily have been mistaken for an ordinary businessman.

The pentagram stopped glowing, and again the cave was plunged into almost complete darkness.

The demon took a step towards Zoran. "For what purpose have you summoned me, witch?" He sounded irritated.

"I have a proposition for you," Zoran replied.

"This better be worth my time," the demon hissed.

Zoran turned to Kees and Sabin. "Leave us. When I need the two of you again, I'll find you."

"Of course," Sabin replied, and bowed his head.

Kees and Sabin vanished a moment later, leaving me alone with Zoran and the demon.

"Andras," Zoran started. "I have . . . an arrangement I'd like to discuss."

"If I were interested in making an *arrangement* with you, as you call it, then I would have sought you out, not the other way around. You may be a powerful witch, but I have no interest in making deals with the Council's little pet."

"That is where you are mistaken," Zoran said. "I am not their little pet, but you are correct in believing that the Council has a certain affection for me, which means they have no reason to suspect that I will be the one to bring them to their knees . . . with your help."

Andras cocked his head to the side and smiled, clearly curious. "What is it they've done to earn your disapproval?"

"I am sick and tired of being bound by their rules. What good is a witch's magic if we aren't allowed to freely use it?"

"And what is it that you want to use your magic for? Hmmm?" Andras looked excited, like he was feeding off Zoran's desires.

"The Wilds needs a new leader." Zoran paused, then finished with a mischievous smile. "Someone who isn't afraid to do whatever it takes to get what they want." He looked different than he had a few hours ago. His hair was no longer tied back, and instead spilled halfway down his back. He'd also changed his clothes and was now wearing a cream-colored tunic style shirt atop dark flowing pants. Neither change made him any less intimidating.

But Zoran's menacing appearance was nothing compared to the demon's. Darkness, fear, anger, hate—they all emanated from him.

"Exactly what is it that you think I can do for you?"

"There is a power I seek. A power I have used every spell I know to obtain, but nothing has worked," Zoran said.

"And what power would that be?"

"I need to learn how to control minds, to make people do as I wish."

Andras tilted his head back and laughed. "Aren't you witches prohibited from using dark magic?" He took a few steps closer to Zoran, a glint in his dark eyes.

Despite the bizarre conversation taking place in front of me I stood still, hoping Andras wouldn't notice me.

"What makes you think that I trust you enough to help you obtain the power you claim to want? How can I be sure you're not just setting me up and that your plan isn't to turn me over to the Council? I'm certain you know they've been hunting me for years."

"I have a gift, a small token to prove my allegiance to you," Zoran said. His lips curled into a smile and then he walked toward me, grabbed my arm, and pulled me until I was face to face with Andras.

"A *girl?*" Andras scoffed. "What do I need with another one of those?"

"Take a closer look."

Andras made a low growling noise before holding one of his hands out, palm up. A glowing ball of light formed and hovered in the air less than an inch over his hand. He took a step closer to me. Dread began to fill my chest until I felt as if I were drowning in it. Zoran had mentioned a gift, he couldn't have meant me. Was I meant to become some sort of demonic sacrifice?

Until that moment, Andras had seemed oblivious to my presence. But, as he studied me, a smile spread across his face and his eyes flashed. "How is she possible?" he asked, staring at me. "I thought Naiara had no children."

"Her father is human," Zoran replied, bitterly. "I only recently learned of her existence."

"Ahhh, I see." Andras grew thoughtful. "The only problem is, if Naiara finds out what you've done with her daughter, she won't be pleased, not with you or with me. Perhaps I should go to her and let her know what you are up to."

"You won't do that," Zoran said, sounding sure of himself, "because if you do, you won't get the girl, *or* my allegiance, and I know you want both."

"She is quite lovely," Andras said. He reached out to touch my cheek.

I moved out of reach before he could.

"I'm not a thing," I stammered, looking between Zoran and Andras. "You can't just hand me over to someone like a piece of property. I won't go anywhere with him."

"Hmmm," Andras said. "She doesn't seem willing."

Zoran smirked. "Since when has that ever stopped you?"

"Did you hear what I said? I'm not going anywhere with him!"

Andras and Zoran ignored me.

"So do we have a deal then?" Zoran asked.

"Not so fast. How do I know I am not being tricked? Perhaps this girl's appearance is just a glamour."

Zoran laughed. "A powerful demon like you, fooled by glamour? Is that even possible? No. Unlike your other wives, with this one, what you see is what you get."

Wives???

"And I'm just supposed to take your word for it?"

Zoran sighed. "I already told you, her father is human; he had no magic and neither does the girl."

"That doesn't mean she has no magic. We both know her mother is one of the most powerful witches in all the worlds. Surely she's inherited something from her."

"The girl is eighteen already. If she had powers, they would have shown themselves by now."

"She's barely eighteen, by the looks of her. And as we both know, the more powerful the ability, the longer it takes to present itself."

"Do I need to remind you again of what her father was?"

"Hmm, I suppose you have a point."

"Whoa, wait just a second," I said as everything that was being said in front of me began to sink in. "I haven't agreed to be anyone's wife." I turned to Andras. "Please. All I want to do is go back home."

"No one is interested in what you want," Zoran spat.

"You don't know what you're doing," I shouted, unable to control my mixed fear and fury. "When my mother finds out, she'll hate you. She'll never forgive you."

"By the time Andras and I have finished our business, I will have acquired the power to make your mother forget all about you and your father. The only man she'll think of is me, and the only love she'll remember is mine. You and your father will cease to exist for her. You won't even be a memory."

"You're wrong. She won't forget about me. Nothing can make a mother forget about her own child," I said as convincingly as I could, even though I wasn't sure it was true.

"Her innocence makes her even more appealing," Andras mused. He took a step back from me.

I turned toward him, desperation overriding my repulsion. "You don't want me. There's nothing special about me. I'm just a boring girl."

"Oh, you have no idea how wrong you are," Andras said, shaking his head. "I haven't felt desire like this for years. A woman with your beauty—I couldn't forget you even if I tried. And the fact that you're a human with no abilities, makes the deal even sweeter. I haven't had a human wife in hundreds of years. It will be so much fun. You are perfectly beautiful and perfectly harmless, a splendid combination. When you are seen by my side, heads will turn and tongues will wag. You will be my wife, my queen, a priceless treasure that everyone covets, but only I possess." Andras turned to

Zoran. "Once our partnership is complete, you will need to be prepared to follow my orders. Is that understood?"

"Of course," Zoran replied, bowing his head. "As long as you keep up your end of our bargain."

"What do you need Zoran for?" I said. "Use the power for yourself to get what you want; just leave me out of this."

"Witches and demons are both powerful creatures, but it's when we combine our magic that we are truly unstoppable. Our magic will feed off each other. Together, Zoran and I will rule the Wilds unchallenged," Andras said.

"Zoran, please." I turned to him. "I'm begging you. Don't do this to me." I felt like I couldn't breathe.

He ignored me.

"I'll need some time to prepare," Andras said. "Have the girl ready for me by tomorrow. After our ceremony, you'll get what you want. Not a minute before."

"She'll be ready."

"I can hardly wait." Andras left us, tossing a satisfied smile our way before vanishing.

"I have some preparations of my own to make," Zoran said. "I'll send Sabin back later with some dinner for you. Be sure to get some rest. Tomorrow is a big day for both of us."

Before I had a chance to reply, Zoran was gone. I turned and let my forehead fall forward against the wall in front of me. Tears I could no longer control sprang from my eyes and ran down my face. I felt like I was choking. What did being a wife to a demon even mean? There was no way I was going to let him touch me. I would rather die.

Die. Perhaps death was my best option, my only way out of this situation. If I died, Andras wouldn't get the bride he wanted. Maybe that would be enough to make him back out of his deal with Zoran, especially if it was Zoran who killed me.

A plan began to form in my mind. When Zoran returned, I'd find a way to provoke him. I would make him so angry that he wouldn't be able to control himself. It was obvious he had temper issues—all I needed to do was push him over the edge. But how?

Time passed slowly, painfully. My head began to hurt again and with the pain came whispers that made me wonder if I got a concussion from hitting my head when Zoran had thrown me across the room. I curled into a ball on the floor, wrapping my arms over my head in the hope that it would help.

Sometime later, Sabin returned with food, the same heavenly smelling meat that Kees had brought earlier. It made my mouth water, but again, I couldn't bring myself to eat. Sabin placed the plate on the floor and left without saying a word.

As minutes turned into hours, my grumbling stomach made the dinner Sabin brought impossible to ignore. I picked at the food, savoring the flavor despite the fact that it had gotten cold. After my hunger abated, I took the plate and hurled it across the room in a fit of anger and frustration.

I sat back down and lowered my head onto my bent knees. I thought about Devin and my mother and wondered where they were. I was beginning to lose hope that they'd be able to find me. If Zoran had gotten to them, there was no way out of this cave.

The pain in my head got worse, and so did the whispering. I cried out and clasped my arms around my head. The pain I could deal with, but the noise was unsettling as it gradually increased in volume. Eventually, the whispering turned into an actual voice and then words. Someone was saying my name. I panicked, even more convinced I had some sort of brain injury, not that it mattered. Nothing mattered anymore.

"Lilli, listen to me."

"Stop it, stop it," I cried. But the noise in my head only got louder. Desperate to drown it out, I was about to scream, when I recognized the voice. I sat perfectly still and listened.

"Tell me where you are."

"Mother?"

"Lilli, listen to me. You're not imaging things. I'm going to find you, but I need your help."

How was I having a conversation with my mother? For almost a week Devin had tried to teach me how to reach her, but I'd never been able to. "I don't know where I am."

"Speak with your mind, not your lips. I can hear you better that way," my mother said. "Now tell me, did Zoran say anything about where he has you, did he give you any clues?"

"No. I asked him, but he wouldn't say. I think he's keeping me in a cave."

"Think, Lilli. Did he give you any clues that might help me figure out how to find you?"

Zoran hadn't, but Kees may have. "One of the men that are helping Zoran said I was in the Void. Is that even a real place?"

A long silence followed and I worried that whatever connection my mother managed to establish had been cut off somehow.

"Good girl," my mother finally said. "It is a real place. Don't be scared. I'll figure out how to find you there. Only . . ."

"Only what?"

"It may take some time to locate you. The Void is a rather big place and enchanted with all sorts of magic. Its paths change at will. But Devin is with me, his ability will help us track you."

"What if you can't?" I asked, hearing the desperation in my voice.

"We will, I promise."

And then the noise in my head went silent.

Chapter 28

NOT HAVING ANY one to talk to or anything to do started to drive me crazy after a while. Hours passed. The cave was cold and dark—I badly wanted a shower and a warm bed. I felt hopeless and desperate. My mother promised she'd find me, but what if it was too late by the time she did?

Eventually, my exhaustion overrode everything else and I fell asleep on the cold, hard ground.

I awoke to find Zoran hovering over me. "You look dreadful," he said as I sat up. "Lucky for you, I've brought something that will help."

A white dress was draped over one of his arms. The fabric shimmered in the candlelight. Zoran held it up, as if proud that he'd managed to find me something so nice.

"You don't honestly think I'll wear that, do you?"

"You can't get married in those clothes," he said, pointing to what I was wearing.

"I'm not getting married to anyone," I hissed at him. "And you can't force me into that dress."

"Maybe Andras will get you to change your mind."

"No. He won't."

"A word of advice, Lilli. You can make things hard for yourself or you can make them easy. You are no match for Andras. He's been around for hundreds of years. He may be infatuated with you now, but force his hand and he will lose his patience and you *will* see his bad side."

"He's a demon; aren't all his sides bad?"

Zoran held the dress out to me as if he expected me to change my mind. I took it from him and held it up, pretending to admire it. Zoran seemed pleased until I bunched up the fabric in my hands, threw it to the ground, and stomped on it over and over again. His eyes flashed with anger as he struck me across my cheek.

My face stung, but it was worth it to see how angry I'd made Zoran. It would be easier than I thought to push him to his limit if the time came. I didn't want it to come to that, though. I wanted to see Devin again. I wanted his arms around me, and I wanted to feel his lips on mine. But the hope I'd felt earlier was beginning to fade. It had been hours since I'd told my mother about the Void, but she still hadn't found me.

"You ungrateful . . ."

"I told you I wasn't going to wear it," I shouted.

"What is all the fuss about in here?"

I recognized the voice. Andras was back, dressed in his finest clothing.

"Zoran just attacked me," I said, pointing an accusatory finger at him.

"She is not yours to touch, Zoran. You promised her to me. Lay another finger on my bride and I will be very unhappy with you."

Stooping to pick up the dress, Zoran didn't respond. The

white fabric had a few streaks of dirt on it, but otherwise it looked fine.

"I brought your bride a dress to wear for your ceremony, but she doesn't seem interested in it."

"There's no need for a fancy dress," Andras said simply. "She looks perfectly lovely the way she is now." He turned toward me. "Are you ready, beautiful one?"

I shook my head. "No. I'm not ready. I'll never be ready. I'm not marrying you, not now, not ever."

"You don't want me?" He sounded offended.

"What she wants isn't important," Zoran said. "And I'm tired of wasting time listening to her complaints. I say we get this over with so we can get on with our plans."

Ignoring Zoran's comment, Andras took a few steps toward me. I backed away, but eventually there was nowhere to go. Trapped against the wall of the cave, I couldn't escape his approach. He stopped and studied me before reaching for my face, brushing his fingers over my lips. I turned my head away, trembling. He smiled, and I realized he enjoyed my fear and revulsion.

"So pretty," he whispered.

I darted under his arm to try and get away. He spun around and grabbed my wrists. His grip was so strong that it felt like he would break my bones. He pulled me toward him, crushing my body against his, and held both of my hands behind my back with one of his. No amount of squirming helped. With his other hand he reached behind my head and drew me close, intending to kiss me. My stomach coiled into a knot and my heart raced in terror at the thought.

"Let go of me," I pleaded. Tears streamed down my face.

Andras laughed. He clearly enjoyed my discomfort. "You're a wild one, aren't you?"

"If anyone can tame her, you can," Zoran said, sounding bored.

His voice made my blood boil. *I will kill him.* In my entire life I'd never hated anyone as much as I hated Zoran.

I struggled to free myself from Andras's grip, but it was impossible. He was far too strong. He moved his hand away from the back of my head and a surge of relief ran through me until he began to trace his fingertips over my cheek. His hand moved slowly down the side of my face, then my neck, and across my shoulder. His hand crept lower and lower until it was almost on my breast. I wanted to scream, to cry, to beg him to stop, but I knew it wouldn't do any good. If anything, he liked to watch me struggle.

I closed my eyes and tried to block his face from my mind, but it didn't help because I could still feel him touching me. I needed to find a way to make him release me from his grip—then I could run; I could get Zoran to chase me until he lost his temper, until I made him angry enough to finally end this horrible nightmare. I let out a cry I didn't even realize I had in me.

A moment later, I felt the pressure on my wrists release. *Run,* my mind told me. I couldn't though; my legs felt too weak. Instead, I backed away from Andras slowly, too consumed in my own terror to notice that something about him had changed.

Andras cried out and I recognized the agony in his voice as my own. He doubled over and fell to his knees as if someone had sucker-punched him.

"What did you do to him?" Zoran said, rushing to his side.

I kept backing away until I hit the wall behind me, and

nearly collapsed the same way Andras had. I watched as he slowly uncurled his body. Pure fright filled his eyes. With his hands off me and some distance between us, my panic subsided and I felt like I could take a breath again.

"What did you do?" Zoran roared.

I was as clueless as he was. "Nothing," I shouted, sure that whatever was going on had nothing to do with me. "I didn't do anything to him."

Andras made it back on his feet. He still seemed shaken, but not like he had a few moments earlier. He didn't look at me, instead he wiped the sweat from his brow, adjusted his tie, and then, as quick as a cat, pounced on Zoran, grabbing him by his neck. "How dare you double cross me?" he asked, his voice as cold as ice.

Zoran couldn't talk. He tried and failed to pry Andras's hands from his neck until somehow, using his power, he was able to force him off.

The demon stumbled over his feet, allowing Zoran to breathe again.

"If you ever try to summon me again, I will kill you," Andras said, his voice full of rage. I watched in disbelief as a ball of flames formed in one of his palms. He hurled it at Zoran, who ducked to avoid being hit.

"I haven't double crossed you," Zoran said. "I swear it."

"You said she had no powers."

"She doesn't!"

"Liar!" Andras's voice boomed. He marched over to Zoran and pushed him against the wall. "How dare you try to make a fool of me?"

"Wait a minute," Zoran pleaded. "Whatever you think she did, you are mistaken. The girl has no powers."

Andras let out a wicked laugh. "You really believe that, don't you?" The look on Zoran's face seemed to answer his question. "A word of advice, keep that girl away from me, and if you know what's good for you, you'll stay away from her as well." He vanished without waiting for Zoran's response.

A sense of relief flooded through me, but the feeling didn't last long. Zoran's face contorted in anger. His eyes blazed and he clenched his jaw. Andras may have left, but my nightmare was far from over.

"What have you done?" he said, his eyes narrowing to slits.

I, too, was beginning to wonder. "I don't know. Maybe your demon friend just realized what you're doing is wrong."

"I can assure you Andras came to no such realization," Zoran scoffed. "He doesn't care about wrong or right—or you, for that matter. You did something to him, and you're going to tell me what."

"I already told you, I didn't do anything."

"You've just ruined everything for me," Zoran said. His murderous gaze locked on me. "Which means I have no more use for you."

With a flick of his hand, he sent me flying across the room like a rag doll. When my body hit the ground it felt like my ribs had shattered. I gasped for air, but before I could catch my breath, Zoran stalked over to me. He knelt beside me, grabbed me by my hair and lifted my head off the ground so he could force me to stare into his cruel face. "I should leave you here to starve to death," he said. "But I'm afraid that Kees will return and rescue you. He likes you, you know, but your pretty face won't be enough to save you."

I was in too much pain to speak. I closed my eyes to block out Zoran's face. He shook my head, and I cried out as I felt strands of my hair being torn from my scalp. "Open your eyes," he demanded.

I refused to obey. My defiance made me feel stronger, even though I knew I stood no chance against Zoran. One more toss across the room would probably mean the end of me.

"I said open your eyes!" he yelled. He let go of my hair and grabbed my neck. His hands tightened. Instinctively, I clutched at them as he choked the life out of me. My time had run out. Everything became hazy except for the pain.

And then it began to ease. I heard screams and muffled voices in the distance, but I couldn't make out any words. The pressure around my neck was gone, and I knew then it was over. I was dead. I heard voices, but whose? My neck felt battered and bruised. I gulped for air and opened my eyes, but something seemed wrong.

I was still in the cave. *This isn't right.* I wasn't sure what happened after a person died, but I liked the idea of Heaven and hoped to wind up there. Except Heaven wasn't supposed to look like this.

"She's ruined everything," someone yelled. It took me a minute to register whose voice it was. Zoran's. But if he was here that meant I wasn't dead. How was that possible? I'd felt him squeezing my life away. Something or someone must have stopped him before he could finish me off.

"No, you're the one who's ruined everything. You ruin everything you touch."

I turned on my side and scanned the room, looking for the person who had saved my life. And then I saw her—my mother, standing a few feet away with Devin beside her. Zoran stood between them and me.

"Lilli." I would have known that voice anywhere.

I wiped my eyes with the back of my hand and managed to use my arms to prop myself up. "Devin."

He darted from my mother's side and ran toward me. I'd never been so happy to see anyone in my life.

But then Zoran spun around.

"I don't think so," he muttered.

Devin's body went flying away from me, too far away to stop Zoran as he pulled me off the floor. "I wasn't finished with you yet."

"Let her go!" my mother demanded.

"Why should I? This girl will cause you nothing but trouble. When the Council finds out about all the rules you've broken . . ."

"I don't care about the Council. I'll take my punishment, but I won't lose my child."

"One day you'll thank me for this."

"No, never!"

Zoran pinned my back against the wall.

My mother screamed as he began to strangle me.

This time my neck would snap, and I had no resistance to offer.

My mother ran over to him and tried to pry him off of me, but he was too strong. "You can't do this!"

"Who's going to stop me?" Zoran's grip around my neck grew tighter. I couldn't yell, I couldn't even talk. For a few precious moments I'd believed I was saved, but I was wrong.

"No, Zoran, you don't know what you're doing," my mother pleaded again, her voice desperate. She dropped to her knees. "She's . . . she's your daughter. You cannot kill our child."

Chapter 29

FOR THE SECOND time that day, I was sure I was dead. I heard more voices, more yelling in the background. Hands reached for me. I kicked them away and screamed.

"Lilli, it's me. It's me." Devin's voice penetrated my panic. My screams turned into sobs as he knelt beside me and reached around me to lift me into his arms.

"What's happening?" I was still disoriented and in pain as it began to dawn on me that for some reason Zoran had let me go, again. But why? Then the answer came to me—the last words that spilled from my mother's mouth before I blacked out. It seemed impossible that Zoran would believe them. There was no truth to them, so why had Zoran let me go? "We need to get out of here before he comes for me again." I doubted I'd survive a third attempt on my life.

"You're going to be fine," Devin whispered as he stroked the back of my head. I trembled in his arms and held on to him tightly, afraid that if I loosened my grip he would be gone. My mother and Zoran stood a few feet away arguing. I didn't want to listen. Their voices were loud and angry. I wanted to block it all out, but when Zoran started to laugh, I couldn't help but lift my head from Devin's chest to see what was happening.

Zoran's laugh matched the satisfied look on his face. He should've been furious with my mother for lying to him yet again, but the murderous gaze that I'd seen in his eyes earlier was gone.

"Of course," he said, when he realized my attention was on him. "It all makes perfect sense now. You did something to Andras. I saw it with my own eyes, but you shouldn't have been able to. Only a powerful witch would have magic strong enough to affect a demon like him. No half-breed could have done to him what you did."

"What did you just say?" My mother grabbed Zoran by his arm and pulled him around to face her. "What did you to do to my daughter?"

"*Our* daughter you mean," Zoran replied angrily. "How dare you keep her from me all these years?"

My mother stared at Zoran blankly without answering his question.

I turned to look at Devin. "What's happening?" I said, wanting him to tell me everything I'd just heard was a lie; that it was my temporary lack of oxygen making me hear things that weren't really being said.

"I don't know." He pressed my head into his chest like he was trying to keep me from seeing something awful, but it wasn't what I was seeing that bothered me. It was the words that had come from my mother's lips.

"Lilli," my mother called to me.

Even though my entire body screamed in pain, I got to my feet and moved toward her, desperately hoping I'd see something in her eyes that told me the only reason she said what she did was so Zoran would spare my life.

My mother held her hands to her chest. "I'm so sorry you had to find out this way."

My heart sank as I considered her words. "But it's not true?" I said, waiting for my mother to give me a sign that she only said what she had to spare my life, but her expression didn't change. Of course she couldn't admit that she lied, with Zoran standing only a few feet away.

"I wish it weren't. I never wanted you to find out, especially like this, but I had no choice."

"Why now? You had eighteen years to tell him and instead you wait until he's about to kill me," I yelled, hoping my words would prove to everyone that it couldn't really be true, that no mother in her right mind would let things get that far.

"Mark was the only father you knew, the father you loved. I didn't want to take that from you. I prayed that Zoran would never learn of you, but if somehow he did I could protect you without ever having to tell you the truth."

I turned back towards Devin and rested my forehead on his chest. "Tell me it's not true," I whispered to Devin. He didn't answer. "Tell me she's lying," I demanded, my voice louder this time.

He cupped the sides of my face and lifted my head so that my eyes could meet his. "I'm sorry, but I don't think she is."

I hated the pity I saw in his eyes. I felt like I was going to be sick. The weight of everything that had happened to me over the past few weeks, was still happening, came crashing down on me.

"NO!" I cried out, shaking my head. Devin's hands fell to his side.

I looked at Zoran, who still wore a smug smile on his face, then at my mother, whose sad eyes were still trained on me.

"Tell him you lied," I begged. "I don't care if he tries to kill me again."

Death felt better than the prospect of having Zoran for a father.

Before she could answer, Zoran spoke. "You are my child. Even if Naiara swore to me now that you weren't, I would know it was a lie. There is much of me in you."

"There is *nothing* of you in me!"

Pain seared through my body and it wasn't coming from my bruised ribs. It was the pain of my heart being shredded into pieces. It was the pain of realizing that my entire life had been a lie. It was the pain of realizing that the father I loved was being replaced by a monster who tried to hand me off to a demon before trying to kill me—not once, but twice.

Anger and agony tore through me. I released it in a piercing cry that echoed through the walls of the cave.

Devin took a few steps back and clutched at the sides of his head as if he were in pain. He fell to his knees.

I stumbled toward him, but he shuffled away as though he feared me.

Of course he did. He'd fallen for me when he thought I was someone else, but now that he knew what I really was, that my father was pure evil, he didn't want anything to do with me.

"Devin, please." I sank to my knees beside him. I had to convince him that I was nothing like Zoran; that I was the same person I had always been. "It's me, Devin. I'm the same Lilli, you have to believe that."

"Arrghh," Devin cried out in pain and fell to the floor. He brought his knees up to his chest like he was trying to curl himself into a ball.

I crouched down and reached for him again. When my hand touched his arm, he looked up at me with torment in his eyes.

"Please don't," he begged. "It hurts. It hurts so bad." He began rocking his body back and forth and muttering softly, "Make it stop, make it stop."

"Devin, what's happening?" Seeing him like that added to the painful mix of emotions that tore at my insides.

He didn't answer, but instead continued to cry out in pain. He flinched every time I reached for him.

I stood and turned toward Zoran who was still standing a few feet away. No longer arguing with my mother, he just stared at me with a look in his eyes I couldn't decipher. I grabbed him by his wrist. "What are you doing to him?" I demanded, angrily.

Like Andras earlier and now Devin, Zoran also fell to his knees. He clutched at his chest and cried out. He began to mutter words that were so broken and anguished that I couldn't recognize them.

Devin and Zoran seemed to be under some sort of spell, but how? I glanced at my mother. She was silent and still on her feet. It had to be her.

"What's happening to them?" I cried.

"I'm fighting it," she said with a pained expression on her face, "but I can feel it, too. I've never been affected by magic this way before."

"What are you talking about?" I asked, stifling the urge to scream.

"You're the one who's doing this, Lilli."

"I'm not *doing* anything."

"You must be some sort of reverse empath," my mother said with a mixture of confusion and awe. "You're casting your emotions outward." She pointed to Devin and Zoran who still sat huddled on the ground. "They feel what you're feeling, all the pain, all the rage, but it's too much for them to bear, because the emotions belong to you, not them."

"You're lying."

I refused to believe I could cause that much pain to anyone. My mother was right about one thing though. My blood was boiling with rage, and it coursed through my body with every beat of my heart. I could feel it, taste it. "Is that the only thing you know how to do, lie?"

"Listen." She took a few steps toward me, but stopped suddenly and clutched at her chest. After a moment she seemed to recover. "Being here, in the Void, it makes magic unpredictable, sometimes magnifying power, sometimes sapping it away completely. You have to get out of here. It's the only way to make this stop. Now! I'll find you wherever you go, I'll come to you and I'll help you, but you must calm down first."

"How am I supposed to leave? If you haven't noticed yet we're in a cave and there is no way out, believe me, I tried looking for one."

"Use your power, Lilli."

"I can't teleport."

"Yes, you can. All you need to do is close your eyes and

focus. Decide where you want to be, and your magic will take you there."

"You don't get it. Zoran put some sort of blocking spell on me . . ."

"The spell won't hold with him in this state, and your magic is stronger than his. That blocking spell can't keep you here."

"I don't believe you. I can't teleport out of here and I can't *make* people feel anything. It's not possible." I started to inch towards Devin to prove to myself and my mother that whatever was happening, it wasn't because of me. I didn't want to believe I was capable of causing the pain I saw etched on his face.

He howled as I approached.

"Lilli, please. I know you love him. He loves you too, but you're hurting him now, whether you want to be or not."

I gritted my teeth. "You did this to me."

"You need to try and calm down . . ."

"Calm down? How am I supposed to do that?" Tears streamed down my face. My chest felt full of daggers that were stabbing me in every direction. Everything in the world that ever meant anything to me was lost.

Out of nowhere, the ground beneath me swayed. Dust and debris rained down from the top of the cave. A crack formed in the ground.

"What the hell!"

"You need to go now, before these walls fall down on us. It's you who's doing this, your emotions, your mind, your power. If you don't leave now, we'll all be buried here."

More dust and rocks fell. A part of me wanted to argue with my mother and insist she was wrong, but what if she wasn't? Anger and pain emanated from me uncontrollably and I knew that she spoke the truth. I'd get us all killed if I couldn't control my power.

There wasn't enough time for me to try and fail. I needed to get out of the cave before I did any more damage. So I closed my eyes. With all the emotions churning inside of me, it was hard to focus. I didn't even know where I wanted to go, but I knew who I wanted to be with. My father, my real father, the one who, for as long as I remembered, always found a way to make things better. I saw his face in my mind, his soft sandy hair and his hazel eyes that sparkled when he smiled, and for a second I felt lighter. A moment later I could feel my body shift as I teleported.

Chapter 30

THE SENSE OF vertigo wasn't as bad this time. Still, I waited to open my eyes until I was sure that I wouldn't keel over. When I did, I found myself in a grassy field dotted with headstones. It took me a moment to realize I had wound up in the cemetery, of all places. I'd been thinking of my father and somehow teleported to his headstone.

I walked toward my father's headstone and rested my hand on the cold granite. "Oh Dad," I murmured, "You don't know how badly I wish you were still here." The words choked in my throat. "I miss you so much. You don't know how much I need you right now. I know you said you believed in me, but you were wrong. My life is a mess, and everything's backwards." I sank to my knees and leaned my head forward until it was almost touching the headstone. With all the crying I had already done, I was sure I wouldn't have any more tears left, but somehow I did.

I lay down on the warm grass in front of my dad's headstone, overcome with sadness and a sense of isolation. I couldn't stand the way I was feeling. The grass under me started to wither and turn yellow and I gasped in shock.

What is happening?

I needed to pull myself together, so I closed my eyes and took long, deep breathes. My mother should've kept her secret. Her confession had saved my life, but maybe my life wasn't worth saving. I'd already lost the only parent I ever knew, and now Devin. What was I even going to do with the rest of my life? My ability would make being around me dangerous. I'd be forced to live my life cooped up inside like a crazy lady.

Eventually, my deep breathing worked and I began to calm down. To my relief, the grass started to turn green again.

I was so very, very tired. In the past two days I'd barely slept, and it had finally caught up with me. I thought to myself that I should go home, get cleaned up, rest and eat, but I wasn't sure how to get there. I'd managed to teleport to my father's grave by thinking of him, but I hadn't planned on the cemetery as my destination. I worried about where I'd wind up if I tried to teleport again. The last thing I needed was to appear in front of people who would totally freak out and who I might accidentally hurt. I had no car with me, no money, and the battery on my phone was dead.

Too tired to come up with a plan, I just lay there. Eventually I'd figure out what to do.

When I opened my eyes sometime later, I was no longer at the cemetery. Somehow I'd managed to make it back home and onto my couch. I sat up, confused and afraid.

"Lilli, it's okay. I'm here." My mother was coming from the kitchen with a cup of tea in her hands. She handed me the cup before kneeling down in front of the couch. "Drink. Everything's going to be okay."

"How did I get here?" I took the tea, but I didn't feel like drinking, so I set it down on the side table.

"You fell asleep in front of your father's grave. I found you and brought you here."

"He's not my father," I said blankly.

"He's your father in every way that matters." My mother reached out to stroke my hair.

"No, he's not," I said, unable to keep the sadness out of my voice.

"You're angry with me?" The way my mother said it made it sound more like a question than a statement, and I wondered how she could think I would feel any other way.

I got off the couch and took a few wobbly steps. She looked upset, but I was too tired and angry to care about her feelings. "Thank you for finding me and bringing me back home, but right now I just want to be alone."

"I know you've been though a lot, but we need to talk . . ."

"I don't *need* anything from you." I turned my back on my mother and crossed my arms.

"Lilli . . ."

And then, because curiosity got the better of me, I turned to ask, "Actually, there is one thing I want to know. Why would you lie about who my father was when you knew what Zoran would do to me? Why did you leave me behind when you could've brought me to the Wilds with you?"

"My vision," my mother replied so quietly I wasn't sure I heard her right.

"What vision?" I asked.

My mother combed her hands through her hair. "The one where I watched you die."

Chapter 31

THAT WAS NOT the answer I'd expected.

"Excuse me?"

My mother sighed. "Like most witches, I got my ability when I was around the age you are now. Ever since I had my first vision, I've wondered whether seeing is blessing or a curse. I suppose it's probably a bit of both."

I sat on the edge of the coffee table as she spoke. "They say that together two powerful witches create an even more powerful child." My mother gave me a weak smile. "That was why my parents and Zoran's arranged for our marriage while we were still in our cradles. I know the idea of an arranged marriage probably sounds horrifying to you, but these arrangements are not unusual among the families of the more powerful witches. Zoran and I grew up together. He was handsome, funny, daring, and brave, and I was in awe of him. He was so young when his father died. His mother didn't know how to be there for him, so I was the one who comforted him. But something about Zoran always scared me a little. Still, I thought I was meant to save him, that I could keep the darkness inside him at bay. Until I started having visions of him with his hands around my neck."

My mother pressed her palm to her forehead and took a deep breath before continuing. "I tried convincing myself that my mind was playing tricks on me, that Zoran loved me, and there was no way he would hurt me, but the visions kept coming, and the more they did, the clearer they became. Eventually, I realized I wasn't seeing Zoran trying to kill me. I was seeing you, the child I would one day have with him. I realized what it meant—that one day he'd give in to the darkness I'd always sensed in him."

My mother's confession had my head spinning.

"Once I grasped what I was seeing, I became determined to change the future. Witches don't have a lot of children. Many try for years before they're able to have even one. Still, I didn't want to take any chances, so I visited a witch skilled in tonics to ask her to make a potion to keep me from getting pregnant. She laughed and told me it was too late, that I already had a child growing inside me. I'd only been with Zoran once, it didn't seem possible, but if it was, I knew I couldn't let him know. I wasn't sure what to do, but I knew I no longer wanted to marry Zoran after what I'd seen him do in my visions. That was when I decided to run away. Without a word to anyone, I fled from the Wilds and found my way to the last place anyone would think to look for me."

"The human world—Crescent City?"

My mother nodded. "I met Mark only a few days after leaving the Wilds. He was on one of his morning jogs and practically ran into me. I loved him from the moment I first laid eyes on him. I know most humans laugh at the notion of love at first sight, but your father was different. Before I left the Wilds, I thought I was love in Zoran, but your father taught me what real love was supposed to feel like. I kept praying that the witch who'd told me I was pregnant had been wrong, but soon enough I realized she wasn't. Eventually, I had no choice but to tell Mark. As soon as the words 'I'm pregnant' came out of my mouth, your father was so over-joyed that I couldn't bring myself to ruin things. He assumed the baby I was carrying was his. The two of us hadn't been together long, but he *wanted* to have a baby with me."

"That doesn't make it right," I said, shaking my head. "You say you loved him, but you lied to him. You let him think that he was my father when he wasn't."

"He was a good father to you, wasn't he?" my mother said. "I can see that you don't approve of what I did, but every-thing would have been fine if only Dara hadn't found me. I bound your powers so that you'd never know about the Wilds or being a witch. I wanted a normal life for you. One without the constant battle between darkness and light that we face in the Wilds. And one where you wouldn't be forced into a mar-riage you didn't want."

I shook my head. "You just don't get it."

My mother furrowed her brows. "What do you mean?

"There had to have been another way to protect me with-out lying to everyone."

"Yes, there was." The tone in my mother's voice shifted. "I could've done what Zoran did and asked a demon to use dark magic to get the life I wanted with you and your father. But doing that would've changed me, I would've no longer been the person your father fell in love with, and I refused to let Zoran and his mother turn me into that."

"You tried to keep me from my destiny, but you couldn't," I said in a whisper.

"I suppose not." My mother lowered her head.

"You don't see it?" I said, dumbfounded by her blindness. "See what?"

"Your vision of Zoran with his hands around my neck," I started. "Have you ever stopped to think that it was all your lies and deceptions that made it come true? Every decision you made brought me closer and closer to that moment when I almost died."

My mother covered her face with her hands and started to cry. "I just wanted to protect you. Some witches say that what you see in a vision can't be changed, but I was determined to keep you alive."

"Did you actually see Zoran kill me in your visions?"

She shook her head. "No, but when you see a man with his hands around your child's neck, what are you supposed to think?"

I sat down beside my mother and circled my arm around her back. Now that I understood why she'd made the decision she had, I realized I had no right to be angry with her. I felt sorry for the choices she had to make at such a young age. And nothing she'd done excused Zoran for trying to hand me over to a demon. "We can't change the past," I said, trying to comfort her the best I could. "No matter how much we wish could."

My mother dried her eyes with the edge of her sleeve and took a deep breath. "You're right, we can't. I know you've been through a lot over the past few days, but things will get better. I saw . . ."

"Please no." I held up my hand to stop her. "I don't want

to know my future, especially if there's nothing I can do to change it. Too much has happened. Between losing Dad, and now Devin . . ."

"You haven't lost him."

She was wrong, I was sure of it, but I didn't feel like talking about Devin.

My mother leaned forward to kiss my cheek. "Get some more rest, my darling Lilli. I'll be back after, and we can talk more then." A moment later, she was gone.

Chapter 32

I HEADED UPSTAIRS, PEELED off my clothes, and stepped into the shower. As the hot water pelted my skin, I began to relax. I did my best to empty my mind. So much had happened, and I was too tired to sort through it all.

When I finished in the shower, I wrapped myself in my bathrobe and went back downstairs to the kitchen. A few boxes of frozen pizza were stacked in the freezer. I placed one in the oven and sat staring outside at my backyard while it baked.

Too impatient to wait for it to cool, I practically burned my tongue as I bit into the first slice. Three slices later I was still hungry, but the sound of someone knocking on the front door made me pause between bites. It couldn't be Katy, she would have just let herself in. Panicked, my mind flashed through the possibilities. Anyone supernatural wouldn't have bothered knocking. I sat there frozen, hoping that who-ever it was would just go away. But they didn't, there was another knock.

The third round of knocking was accompanied by a voice.

"Lilli, it's me. I know you're in there. Open the door, please," Devin pleaded.

At the sound of his voice, my heart shattered into a million pieces. I rose from my chair and started for the door, my need for him intense. Halfway there, I stopped. I wanted to open the door and run into his arms, but I was afraid. For a minute I considered pretending I wasn't home, but I knew that wouldn't do any good. He could probably hear me from where he was.

"Go away," I shouted. It hurt to say those words, they were the last thing I ever wanted to tell him, but the look of agony on his face from earlier was etched into my mind. I refused to cause him pain like that again.

"I'm not going anywhere." His voice sounded as tortured as I felt, and I was afraid that it was me hurting him all over again. "I'll stay out here all night and all day and the day after until you open this door and let me talk to you."

"I don't want to hurt you again," I said, trying to be strong, not only for myself, but for him, too.

"The only thing that hurts is being away from you. Please, just let me in," he pleaded. "You won't hurt me. I can help you. I can teach you how to control your power."

"No."

"Lilli, please . . . I need you. I can't breathe without you. I love you." His voice cracked and I wondered if I'd heard him right, but then he said it again, and again, and again.

Forgetting everything else, I ran to open the door and threw myself into his arms. Relief flooded through me as he wrapped his arms around me. I seriously doubted I'd ever be able to let go again.

Devin scooped me up into his arms and carried me inside.

He kicked the door shut behind him and laid me down on the couch. "Tell me I'm not dreaming," he said as he stared at my face. "I thought I'd lost you forever. Tell me I haven't."

His lips were on mine before I had a chance to answer him. *No,* I wanted to say. *This is definitely too real to be a dream.* His kiss seemed endless, like he was afraid if he stopped, I would disappear.

"I'm not going anywhere," I whispered into his ear. His lips returned to mine as soon as the words were out of my mouth. I groaned, feeling a mixture of pleasure from his kisses and pain from my bruised ribs.

I must have flinched because he pulled away. "Are you all right?"

"I'm fine, more than fine, now that you're here."

He rested his head on my chest, and I liked the way his soft hair tickled my neck. I watched as his back rose and fell with each breath. The rhythm of it soothed me, as did the knowledge that perhaps I was soothing him right back, thanks to my newly acquired power.

"I almost forgot how beautiful you are," Devin murmured as he looked up at me. He closed his eyes and inhaled deeply. "And how delicious you smell." When he opened his eyes I felt his lashes brush softly against my neck.

Then he arched away from me abruptly.

"This is what Zoran did to you, isn't it?" he said through gritted teeth as his fingers stroked my neck.

I reached for his hand, which was still touching my neck. Of course there would be marks there. I hadn't bothered looking into any mirrors since I'd managed to barely escape with my life. I nodded, trying desperately to push away all thoughts of my struggle with Zoran. I had never been so aware of my own emotions, but now that I knew the damage they could do, I didn't have any other choice.

"We don't have to talk about it now," Devin said, sensing my unease.

"You don't hate me?"

His kiss said he didn't, but a part of me feared that when he really thought things through, he would realize that being with me wasn't what he wanted anymore.

"Hate you?" He frowned. "How could I ever?"

"I hurt you earlier." My voice dropped. "I didn't mean to. I'm sorry. I didn't even know what I doing until my mother said it was me. I still can't believe that I can do something so . . . horrible."

"Shhh. We don't need to worry about that right now. You didn't mean to hurt me; I know that. If anyone is to blame, it's Zoran. The stress that he put you under is what made everything happen the way it did, and being in the Void didn't help either."

"What is the Void exactly?"

"It's a no man's land between worlds. Magic tends to be a little unpredictable there."

A no man's land; it felt a lot like that when I was there. All I knew was the Void was one place I never wanted to go back to, or think about. "Can I ask you something?"

"Anything."

"Do you hate me because of who my . . . father is?" I almost choked on the words.

"Did you hate me after I told you about my father?"

I shook my head. "You know I didn't."

"Zoran wasn't the one who raised you. You're nothing

243

like him. Just because he's your father, it doesn't change who you are."

"So you think my mother was right for lying to my dad and letting him think he was my real father?" I asked.

"No . . . yes," he stuttered. "I don't really know. But what I do know is that if she hadn't, we would never have found each other, and right or wrong, I can't be sorry about the way things turned out."

"You don't think we would have found a way to each other if we'd grown up together?"

He shook his head. "No. Zoran would've forbidden you from being with me."

"Because your father is a shapeshifter?"

"Yes."

I didn't argue with him, although I was sure he was wrong about us not being able to find a way to be together. I couldn't see the future the way my mother could, but it felt like Devin and I were destined to be with each other.

"You look tired," Devin said. "Let me bring you upstairs."

I shook my head. "I don't want to sleep. I want to be with you."

"I'm not going anywhere," Devin said, stroking my cheek. "After what you pulled, leaving me back in Kansas City the way you did, I doubt I'll ever let you out of my sight again."

"I'm sorry. I thought . . ."

"I'm not angry with you, if that's what you're thinking. I'm too happy to have you back in my arms to think about anything else," Devin said. "Perhaps it's for the best. If I let myself think about Zoran with his hands around your neck . . ." He shook his head like he was trying to clear the memory from his mind.

"I don't want to think about that either. I'm worried that if I do I'll hurt you again."

"No. It's different now. You know what you can do, so you can control it. With time you'll be able to use your power to do amazing things."

"How did you know I was here?" I asked, changing the subject. The thought of my ability was still too frightening and overwhelming.

"Your mother told me."

"Did she tell you anything else?"

"Like what?"

"Like about her vision?"

"What vision?"

"It's not important," I said. I wasn't up for any more serious conversation. "I thought you wanted to take me upstairs."

Devin stood and held his hand out to me. I took it and followed him to my bedroom. I lay down on my bed and Devin settled in beside me wrapping his arms around me as I rested my head on his chest.

We lay there quietly for a few minutes until Devin broke the silence. "Lilli, we have something important to talk about."

"No more talking," I said. I pulled Devin closer and pressed my lips on his. My hands slid under his shirt and I stroked every inch of his chest. I climbed on top of him, and let my lips travel down to his neck, smiling as he groaned softly with each contact my lips made with his skin. I wanted more. I lifted his shirt so I could kiss his chest. My tongue darted in and out of my mouth as I let myself taste him. From the way Devin's chest rose and fell I could tell he was breathing fast. Every time I found a new spot to kiss, he arched his back and moaned. His skin felt silky and warm under my hands. I wanted him to touch me the way I was touching him. I wanted to be as close to him as it was possible for two people to be. There was nothing but my robe between us. I reached for the belt at my waist and began to unknot it.

Devin's eyes flew open and he inhaled sharply. "You have to stop, Lilli," he said drawing the edges of my robe back together

"I don't want to stop," I said. "I want you to see me and touch me; all of me."

"Lilli, no. I already told you, once I do those things I'm afraid I won't be able to pull myself away from you. I don't want to do the wrong thing."

"You won't do the wrong thing," I said. "I want you."

"Don't say that unless you're sure," he whispered. "I can wait as long as you want. It'll be hard, next to impossible, but I'd do anything for you."

"I almost died today, twice," I reminded him as I bent forward to kiss his lips. He shuddered and moaned as I pulled off my robe and pressed my naked flesh to his. "I don't want to waste any more time."

Devin threw my robe on the floor. He flipped me onto my back and pulled his shirt over his head. Despite how badly I wanted him, I was nervous and a little afraid. Somehow he must have sensed that so he took his time with me. I reminded myself to breath as he made me feel things I had never imagined were possible.

Chapter 33

AFTER WE HAD made love, I trembled in Devin's arms. "Are you okay?" he asked.

I turned my head to look up at him and smiled, unable to hide how incredibly blissful I felt. "More than okay," I replied resting my chin on his chest. "You're the only good thing in my life, did you know that?"

"You deserve more than just me."

"No. You make up for everything I lost. You're the only one I need . . . I love you." It was the first time I'd had the courage to tell him.

"Do you?"

As I nodded, he smiled and kissed my forehead. "Never let me go, Lilli," he said with a far off look in his eyes.

"Hey," I whispered. I waited for his eyes to meet mine. "I'm yours and you're mine, for as long as you want."

"Forever is what I want."

"That's good." I smiled. "I guess that means we both want the same thing."

We lay quietly. I was tired, but I didn't want to sleep. I was afraid that when I woke up in the morning everything would be different, and I liked the way things were right at that moment.

"Lilli," Devin whispered. "There's something important that I really want to talk to you about."

My lips grazed his chest. "What is it?"

"I want to return to the Wilds, but only if you will go with me." I lifted my head. "And before you say no, you have to hear me out. Your ability isn't exactly the easiest to keep hidden. We could stay away from other people until you learn to control it, but I'm not sure how long it would take. Then there's Zoran to think about. I have no idea what his plans are—he disappeared after you left—but you're his daughter and he will seek you out again. It will be easier to protect you back home."

"What am I going to tell Katy?" I asked. "I can't just disappear; that wouldn't be right."

"We'll think of something," he assured me. "I'm sure she anticipated that one day you'd leave Crescent City."

"Yes, but . . . what about when she tries to call me, or if she wants to visit?" I asked.

"That's something we can work out after you agree."

I looked into Devin's eyes, the ones that made me feel like diving in without caring whether or not I would drown. A week ago, I'd had my doubts about ever returning to the Wilds, but despite everything, I knew it was where I was supposed to be. Devin probably thought it would be a hard decision for me to make after everything that had happened, but it wasn't. Crescent City hadn't really felt like home ever since my dad died. The idea of continuing to live in my house didn't feel right anymore. The memories were painful enough before, but now, after everything that had happened, things were even harder. Knowing the truth didn't make me love the man I called Dad my whole life any less. If anything I loved him more, because he'd raised me and loved me even though I wasn't his. He hadn't known it, but I had a feeling that even if he had, he wouldn't have done anything differently.

"We can't leave until I at least get a chance to say goodbye to Katy."

Devin's lips curled into a smile so big it nearly filled the entire room. He pulled me into his arms and I found myself smiling, too, and not just because Devin was, but because we were going back to the Wilds again. Together.

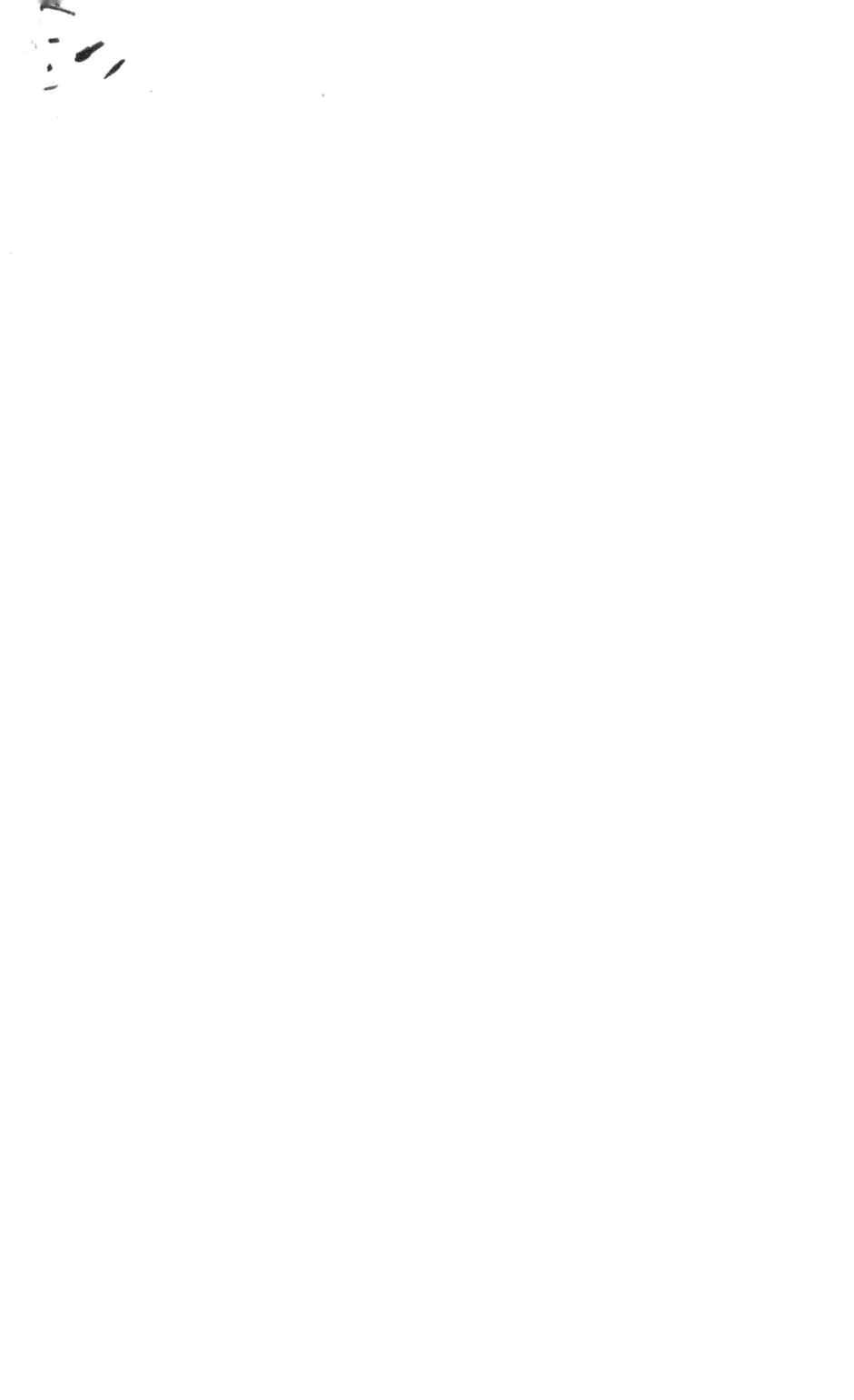

Acknowledgements

I've been working on Daughter of Magic for three years. Although it isn't my first published book, it is the first book I started writing. That's one of the reasons it's so special to me. Daughter of Magic has undergone many re-writes, edits and even title changes until I felt that it was just right. I hope you enjoyed reading it as much as I enjoyed writing it.

Thank you to my husband, Ben, for your support. Thank you to my children who talk about my characters, Lilli and Devin, as if they were real people. They are the best little cheerleaders a mother could wish for. Thank you to my sister, Elisabeth, for reading so many versions of this book, for your edits, for helping me find beta readers and for just being there.

A big thanks also goes to Jennifer Skutelsky for her amazing job editing this book. She really helped me to shape it in to something I could be proud of, and I am in awe of her talent with the written word. I would also like to thank Damonza for creating my beautiful book cover. Their designers really know what they're doing. Finally, I would like to say thank you to all my readers, I hope this book brought a little joy into your lives.

About the Author

Teresa Roman is a lover of books, she loves the way they can take you to a different time and place. Born in Romania, she moved to the states as a young child and has lived on both coasts and the Midwest. Now, she happily calls Sacramento, CA her home, where she lives with her husband, three kids and a dog. When she isn't at her day job or running around with her children, you can find her in front of the computer writing, or with her head buried in another book. You can read more about Teresa at www.teresaromanwrites.com, where you can also sign up for her newsletter to receive the latest news about book releases and giveaways.

Other Titles by Teresa Roman

Back To Us

Connect with me online:

www.teresaromanwrites.com
tromanwrites@gmail.com
https://www.facebook.com/teresaromanauthor
http://www.amazon.com/Teresa-Roman/e/B011K661DC/
ref=ntt_dp_epwbk_0
https://www.goodreads.com/author/show/14163515.
Teresa_Roman

Printed in Great Britain
by Amazon